LEAP OF FAITH

Karena Moss

DEDICATION

To my kids.

CHAPTER 1

I expected to be "that" mom. You know, the mom who volunteered weekly (if not more) in their child's classroom. The mom who the teacher relied on to coordinate birthday parties, classroom celebrations, field trips, etc. The mom who the teacher counted on to help with the mass of paperwork generated by the students on a daily basis. The mom who was just another body in the classroom ready and able to assist during art project day or science fair day. The mom who came to school in her pajamas and read to every kid in the classroom on National Read to your Kid Day. I was going to be "that" mom, and I was going to be great.

***

5:30 a.m.

The white noise coming through the baby monitor was drowned out with the twangy sounds of the local country music station from the alarm clock on my nightstand. *Oh, good grief, I'm exhausted*, I thought. *Twelve weeks in with baby #3 but who is counting? Shouldn't I feel more rested by now? Please Jesus give me energy today as it is…* my brain suddenly triggered alarms to wake up. Bolting upright in bed, now completely awake and fueled with excitement, I quietly shrieked, "First day of school!" I quickly got out of bed, showered, and dressed. With dripping hair and half my make-up on I quietly crept down the hall to Sam's room to wake him up. As I opened the door, I saw Sam scurrying around his room getting dressed. He too seemed excited and suddenly my heart ached. As I silently watched Sam, all my excitement for school seemed to dissolve in one moment. My son. My firstborn. My heart. Today was the day I was going to leave him in someone else's capable hands (or so I had hoped) to learn and grow away from me. Suddenly he looked so young and so incredibly little. For a brief moment, I was no longer excited but seriously devastated. I wanted to cry. But not just cry but to ugly cry! I didn't want my son to go!! Whose stupid idea was it to send small children no taller than a kitchen countertop off to an institution to sit and learn and perform? On the very edge of complete despair and panic, with tears starting to well in my eyes and my brain shouting, *"No! You are not going to school today or ever!"* Sam turned around and with a sleepy grin and said, "Good morning Mom."

Instantly my tears absorbed back into my eyes and with the talent honed from the ancestors of mothers everywhere I walked toward him, wrapped my arms around him, kissed his head with ease, and said, "Good morning sweet pea. First day of school!! Are you super excited?" *Who in the world is this woman talking and where is her voice coming from*, I wondered because I was in no way calm or easy-going-stupid-happy right now! But autopilot obviously had taken over my body like the body snatchers of old because I continued in my drippy happy supportive state. "You must be since I didn't even have to wake you up to get ready for school this morning. You look awful handsome in your school uniform. I was just going to finish getting ready and then go downstairs to make breakfast and your lunch. See you downstairs in a few minutes." And with that I bolted. I heard Sam murmur "ok" as I headed to the sanctuary of my bedroom. As I looked at myself in the mirror in my bathroom my eyes screamed, *"What is wrong with you?*

Get it together. You are excited! Yes, you will miss him but he's growing up and that in itself is exciting!! Remember, you will be the room mom, and all will be great."

As I was finishing up my pep talk, Leah, Sam's younger sister, staggered into the bathroom with her teddy in hand. "Up Mamma. Please."

Forgetting all about my massive meltdown, I scooped up Leah and kissed her cheeks. "Good morning, sweet girl. I missed you all night! Where were you?"

Squeezing her tighter and tickling her neck with kisses, she giggled, "I was sleeping Mamma."

"Well, I'm sure glad it's morning and we get to spend the day together. Why don't you go downstairs, and I'll be there in a minute. Let me finish getting ready real quick."

Grabbing my cheeks in her tiny hands Leah said, "Ok Mamma but can I watch cartoons please?"

"Absolutely. But only for a little bit because we have to take Sam to school today, so I'll need you to get dressed before we leave, ok?" Putting Leah down I watched her walk away with her bear to her nose, waving at me. My heart was full. *Lord, please protect my children. Put your arms around them and let them know how much you love them. Give me strength today and always and guide me to follow your will. In Jesus name, Amen.*

CHAPTER 2

6:45 a.m.

"Let's go! Hurry up or we will be late. Leah, no, you have to leave your bear at home. Yes, you can bring your juice. Did you go potty? Yes, you need to go potty before we leave. I don't want to take you to the bathroom when we get there."

"Sam! Come on honey, you do not want to be late for your first day of school. Peyton said he would wait for you by your room door so you could go onto the playground together." Breathing out slowly I scanned the hallway to make sure I didn't forget anything. "Ok. So, you have your backpack. You have your lunch sack. Your water bottle is inside your lunch sack. Wow. Ok, so that's everything, right?"

"Mom, I'm ready. Let's go. Remember what Peyton's mom said about the traffic?"

"Right. Ok, everybody in the car. Leah, do you need help with your seatbelt?"

"I'm three, Mom. I'm a big girl now."

"Yes, you are. Ok, then, 35 minutes until the bell rings." We pulled out of the garage and onto Agua Azul Street which led to Sunset Blvd. All my anxieties from earlier seemed to have faded away in the hustle of the morning and now I was focused on the task at hand. My friend Julie had warned me that traffic on Sunset Blvd was a parking lot, so I hoped that we had left early enough to avoid that hassle. As we breezed down Agua Azul Street, I started to get cocky. I glanced at the clock.

6:55 am.

Plenty of time to drive 3 miles. As we rounded the corner, I came to a stop in order to turn right onto Sunset Blvd. *What in the world?* I thought to myself. The line of cars extended all the way from my left to my right as far as I could see. As I stared in disbelief, I heard a honk coming from the car to my left waving me into the line. I absent-mindedly waved back, and I pulled into "the parking lot."

7:20 a.m.

I spotted my friend Julie in front of the

building where the kindergarten classrooms were located as the kids and I came running down the breezeway. Having the classroom doors on the outside of the buildings was still new to me since my schools growing up never had outside access. It seemed strange and I wondered about the safety of an outside access opening to an open campus, but my thoughts were interrupted as Julie met me with a hug.

"You made it!! I was starting to get worried. The bell rings in 5 minutes."

"The 'parking lot' was an excellent description. How did you make it here so early? What time did you leave your house?" I asked.

"Well, remember I live a little closer than you do, but we left the house at 6:45. Peyton, why don't you and Sam go play for a few minutes before the bell rings. Mrs. Smith and I won't leave until after you have lined up with your class and are headed into the building."

"Awesome! Let's go Sam!" exclaimed Peyton. Sam followed, and they ran off toward the playground. As I turned to watch the boys run off, my jaw fell open, and panic started to rise again. Looking out onto a sea of heads, I watched my son disappear. The teachers at Kindergarten Roundup had mentioned that about 685 kids from kindergarten to 2nd grade all played on one playground in the mornings. I suddenly wanted to cry again. Instinctively pulling Leah closer to me, I searched the heads for Sam. All I could see was a mass of brown and black hair, and then I saw him! His little toe head kept popping up like popcorn in a kettle. Relieved I could see him, I turned my attention to Julie who had been talking since the boys left.

"So, what do you think? Am I crazy? You must think I have lost my mind since you haven't said anything this entire time."

Having no idea what she was talking about I apologized and asked, "I'm so sorry. I was so focused on the mass of heads swimming out there and trying to spy Sam that I didn't hear a word you said. Please tell me again."

"Yeah, it's a little overwhelming out there, isn't it? There are five playground aids out there watching and a fence along the back of the playground protecting the school from the traffic. They will be fine. I promise. I was actually telling you that there is a kindergarten position that just opened up, and I was thinking about applying for the job. It's been awhile since I had my own classroom, but I think it's a good idea for me to start thinking about getting back into the work force. Jeff's job is so unstable right now, and we seem to always be on budget lockdown. So, I thought it might be a good thing. I know it's a long shot, but I feel that I should give it a try."

"Wow! Yeah, well, I think that sounds like a great idea. Why is there a position available now? School just started?"

"I know, crazy, right? Apparently, there are so many kids enrolled in the primary school this year that they need to open up another classroom. It feels like an answer to prayer, but we'll see if I get the job. So, what do you think?"

"I think that you should give it a shot. If God doesn't want you to take this path, then he will shut the door. Does Peyton know?"

"I talked to him about it last night, and he seemed really excited about his mom being on campus with him. Would you be willing to take Peyton home some days if he doesn't want to hang out with me until I am ready to go home? Jeff will be there working so all you have to do is drop him off."

"Absolutely! Let me know how I can help." Just then the bell rang, and it seemed as though chaos turned into CHAOS.

Leah said, "Um, Mom?" and started backing in closer to me, which looked more like her climbing up my leg, just as a wave of kids started to swarm in our direction. Julie, Leah, and I instinctively stepped back, and teachers seemed to appear from nowhere lining up along the breezeway with huge signs indicating their name and grade. The aids (all five of them which did not seem like enough) started herding the children out in the battlefield into their appropriate lines, and the chaos started to resemble confused order. I saw Sam and Peyton rush up to the line that was forming for their class, and I waved. Sam leaned over to Peyton, said something, and then bolted out of line towards me and Leah. I stepped forward and caught him in a bear hug.

Talking into my cheek, he reassured me,

"Don't worry Mamma. I'll be fine. I'll see you after school. I love you!" And just as quick as he came, he darted back to the line.

"I love you too! Have a good day!" I yelled, but the sea of kids swallowed my words.

CHAPTER 3

106 degrees

I glanced at my watch. 2:00 p.m. *Lord have mercy*, I sighed to myself. *Five more minutes before the doors will open. Maybe my shoes will have melted to the pavement before we get in there.*

"Mamma, I'm hot. When can we get Sam?"

Trying to sound like I was coping well with standing outside in the blazing sun in the parent pick-up line, I said cheerfully, "I am hot too, but I think we only have to wait 5 more minutes. Then the doors will open, and we can go into the gymnasium and pick up Sam." *That is if we don't die of heat stoke out here*, I thought. Turning to look at Leah's bright red, shining face, I prayed the 5 minutes would pass quickly.

As the line finally started to move slowly and we inched closer to the kindergarten pick-up table, I tried to ignore the sweat running in little rivers down my back and instead focus on hearing about Sam's first day. Finally, our turn came and I stepped quickly up to the table.

"Name?" the teacher's aide shouted.

"I'm sorry, what?" I asked.

"Name?" she shouted again.

"Sam Smith!" I shouted back.

I could see Sam sitting on the floor not two feet from me waiting patiently. I smiled and waved to him just as the aide turned her back to me and yelled into the group of kids, "Sam Smith! Your mom's here!" Not expecting her booming announcement Leah and I both jumped. The aid turned back around and yelled, "You need to sign your name next to his on this piece of paper showing you picked him up." Then seeing Sam had answered her loud summons, I quickly signed my name and she brusquely said goodbye. Seeming to have a mind of its own, the line gently pushed us to the side and towards the door. The three of us made a beeline through the exit and escaped into the heat.

As silence engulfed us, it felt only natural to whisper, "So, how was your day?" I asked.

We all cracked up laughing as we headed to the car.

***

Two weeks into August I finally received THE email I had been looking for every day since orientation.

Dear Mrs. Smith:
Since you are the only parent who volunteered to be room mom, I guess the job is yours. If you are available to help Wednesdays and Fridays that would be great. There might be other days and times you could help too, but I'll let you know. Thanks.
Sincerely,
Ms. Thomas

I wasn't sure whether to be overjoyed or suspicious that no one but me volunteered to be room mom. I mean as far as parent roles in the classroom go this was by far THE MOST IMPORTANT. Putting away my trepidations, I found my calendar and started to write in the days Leah and I would be in the classroom with Sam. I was so grateful that Ms. Thomas chose Wednesdays and Fridays as volunteer days since Leah's dance class met on Tuesdays. *Hopefully she enjoys being in the classroom as much as I will*, I thought.

Just then Leah came twirling and leaping into the kitchen. "Mamma, are you ready? I have dance today remember? Do you think everyone will be a better dancer than me? I hope I can meet a friend. I hope you can meet a friend too, Mamma."

Since moving here in November of last year making friends for all of us had been a little rough. We had finally found a church home last month, but friendships were hard to make for some reason. Now that Sam had started school, we were all hopeful that we would meet some families like us.

Putting away the calendar I picked up the hairbrush laying on the counter and started to brush Leah's hair into a ponytail. "You know what Leah? I think we should pray before going to dance."

"Let me Mamma!" Bowing her little head, she began, "Dear Jesus, thank you for loving us. Help me dance good today in class.

Please, Jesus, bring us some friends to play with. In Jesus' name, Amen."

"Perfect! Now, let's get to dance and meet some friends!"

CHAPTER 4

As I was unsure which multipurpose room located inside our community center housed Leah's dance class, we decided to follow the little stream of other girls dressed in pink leotards and chiffon skirts hoping to arrive at our predetermined destination. Noticing that friendships between the girls and their moms had been formed previously, I prayed that Leah would be included and not left out. When the group filed through a door with glass windows on either side, I looked at Leah and said, "Looks like this is where the class is. Let's go in and meet your instructor." Standing in the midst of a group of girls who were obviously "groupies," I spotted the instructor listening to the girls' stories of summer while holding her two-year-old in her arms. Looking very bohemian in design with a hint of hippy grunge, I wondered if we were in ballet or modern dance class. As I stood pondering if I was lost, I watched the instructor put her child down and noticed the dried snot and food on her face. Suddenly I wondered if I should take Leah and run as my inner germaphobe came leaping out.

"You need to expose your children to germs, disease, and sickness," the doctors had told me. "The more germs they are exposed to the healthier they will be." *Yeah, well if they don't die first!* Reigning in my germaphobia and deciding I didn't need to meet the instructor in case this was the only class we would be attending, I looked at Leah and said, "Ok, well, have fun. I'll be right outside the door, so I can watch you. I love you. See you in 30 minutes." As I kissed her and started to walk away, I turned around in a last-ditch effort to make sure she didn't contract some life-threatening disease and suggested, "Remember to keep your fingers out of your mouth." *Like that will help at all,* I thought as I passed a little dancer with a glob of green snot stretching from her nose into her mouth. Feeling the vomit rise, I tried to convince myself that this dance class was a good idea.

Walking out of the classroom door I scanned the waiting area for a place to sit. There seemed to be 3 distinct groups, well 2 if you didn't count the group that only consisted of one woman and her baby. The group to my far left were mostly overweight women with some younger children in their midst. As I was looking in their direction, their circle of friendship seemed to tighten as one would tug on a pull cord to close a bag. Obviously that group was not accepting new members. My gaze shifted to the group directly in front of me. I instinctively smoothed my shirt over my thick pregnant stomach as I suddenly became very body conscious. This was the fit group. Actually, I don't think "fit" accurately described them. Dressed in the proverbial leggings and sports bra with a loose tank top (like that really added any measure of modesty), these women made fitness an occupation. Because owning and flaunting muscles was a job, having only one child was a necessity to "manage the damage" of child rearing. Maintaining their body image took too much time and any more children risked ending up in the fat women's group. They were tight, tucked, plucked and perky. Not sure what parts were real or fake and totally convinced that I couldn't afford to keep my lips bathed in such high reflective gloss, I decided to turn my attention to the 3rd "group."

"Hi, my name is Kit. This is my daughter Leah's first dance class. May I sit next to you?"

In a syrupy southern drawl, the woman

responded, "Well hi! Certainly. I'd love the company. I'm Sally and this is my son David. My daughter Emily is in this class too. She's five. How old is Leah?"

Thank you, sweet Jesus! She seems normal! I silently celebrated. "She is three, almost four, and going on thirteen. We've had a hard time finding something she enjoys doing. Hopefully, the kids actually do some dancing. Because she's not 4 years old yet we've had trouble finding groups that aren't glorified play groups or romper rooms. How old is David? He looks pretty new."

"He is 4 weeks old as of yesterday, and he is giving me a run for my money. My daughter was a walk in the park compared to this little guy. He refuses to sleep through the night, mostly just fussin' and want'n to be awake. It's a killer since I don't get much opportunity to nap during the day with school and all. It looks like you'll be expecting another soon. Will this be your second?"

"No, this will be my third. I have an older boy who is in kindergarten this year. He is at Desert Elementary School. I understand fussy babies. Sam was so colicky. I remember wondering if I'd survive. You mentioned naps were hard because of school. Where does Emily go to school?"

"Oh, we homeschool. Of course, there are a bunch of curriculum options to choose from, but we use Abeka Academy and just love it."

"Oh, how wonderful," I said. *Maybe not so normal after all*, I thought. Not really knowing what else to say, I asked, "Did you always want to homeschool?"

"Yes, I knew from the beginning that I wanted to homeschool my children. Not everyone can do it though. It is truly a calling."

Well, that's for certain, I thought to myself. "What grade is Emily in? Or do you not do grades? Is it expensive? I'm sorry, just ignore me if I am asking too many questions."

"Not to worry. I enjoy talking about homeschooling. I started Emily with the pre-K Abeka program, and now she is in kindergarten. She's been a little challenging this year, but I would guess it's because she has to compete with David for attention. She really hates math but loves to read, so we do a lot of reading together. Honestly, I think homeschooling is a heck of lot cheaper than any private school. You know I think I have a brochure in my bag that came in the mail yesterday." Bending over, Sally retrieved a catalog and handed it to me. "Here you go, that should answer some questions for you. I think I paid a little over $600.00 for kindergarten this year. The price jumps to a little over $800.00 in first grade and then jumps again in ninth grade to a little over $1,000.00. I just love the program though. The materials are so thorough and the presentation of curriculum on the video instruction, if you choose to do those, are incredibly good. The video instruction does add cost though, just so you know. You should look into it for Leah and get a head start on school."

$600-$1,000? Yikes! I can't pay that kind of money. That's crazy. Who does that? Since it would seem rude to say what I was really thinking, I offered an awkward "thank you" and mumbled, "Yeah, I'll check into that. It really sounds great." Thankfully, a gaggle of girls erupted out of the classroom, and I hurriedly exclaimed, "Oh, class is

over. Well, we'd better get home to eat lunch before we have to go pick up Sam from school. It was great to meet you Sally. See you next week!" And with that I took Leah's hand, and we headed towards the exit doors.

"Bye Emily!" Leah exclaimed.

"Bye Leah! See you next time!!"

"Mamma, did you know that Emily homeschools? What does that mean? Will you homeschool me? Emily says it's lots of fun, and we could play with each other all the time. I think we should homeschool, so Emily and I can play together."

Not if I'm going to win the "Room Mom of the Year Award," I thought. "I think you can play with Emily without us having to homeschool, honey. It sounds expensive, and I thought you wanted to go to school with Sam when you turned five years old?"

"I guess. But I still think it would be fun to play with Emily all the time."

Well, not for $600.00.

CHAPTER 5

"Apparently kindergarten only costs a little over $600.00. I can't imagine. That seems really expensive given the fact that we are already paying for public education through our taxes. I just don't understand why she feels called to homeschool. Is there something wrong with the schools here? We looked at the testing scores before we moved to this neighborhood, and they were high. Sam's teacher seems competent even though the school is a little dumpy and old. Should I be more interested in this homeschool thing? My goodness I would have no idea what to teach or how. I'm probably the most inept person to homeschool on the planet. I think I can honestly say that I've never met a 'homeschooler' before. She really was surprisingly normal though."

My husband just stared as I ranted about my morning encounter with the "homeschool" lady. My barrage of words had been ongoing since he walked through the door. It seemed clear that he really had no idea what to say, so he settled on, "Well, I think where Sam is going to school is just fine. If you want to buy some preschool books at Barnes and Noble or Costco or something for Leah to work in, that seems reasonable, but I think spending even $500.00 on preschool curriculum is a bit too much."

"That's what I thought, Matt, but I tell you, she just beamed about it! She totally made me feel like I was missing out on something."

"Well, I don't think you are missing anything. You said that you really think Sam's teacher is good with the kids even though her adult skills are lacking. It's just a lot to take in right now. We've only been here 6 months, we have a baby coming, and our oldest just started school. It'll all be ok."

"I know it will all be ok. But I want more than just 'ok.' Somehow after meeting Sally, I feel different. What if God is trying to tell me something I am unwilling to hear? You know how God works; he puts people in your life and uses them to give you a message He wants you to hear. I mean, I really liked her, and I think we could be friends, but I prayed to meet someone who had kids in public school so our kids would have something in common. And what does He send me? A homeschooler!"

***

"Come on Leah! We're helping for the first time in Sam's class today, and I don't want to be late. Mrs. Thomas is counting on us. We are drawing life-size outlines of our bodies today and then gluing on our organs where they belong."

"I can't find my sandals Mamma. Ooo, do you think Ms. Thomas will let me make my body too?"

"I found them!!" Racing over to Leah with sandals in my hands that I had just located outside in the yard, I bent down only to discover that my arms had apparently shrunk in size. *Oh, for pity's sake*, I thought. Re-arranging myself onto my knees so I could reach Leah's feet, the baby decided to launch a swift kick to my bladder. Standing up suddenly, I dropped Leah's sandals on the floor and walked quickly to the bathroom.

"You just went potty Mamma. Hurry up we are going to be late."

"I know, but your sister has decided to jump on my bladder. I'll hurry; I promise."

"Okay Mamma. I'll get my sandals on." And with that announcement she sat down and diligently put her shoes on. "Oh, look Mamma! I got them on! I'm ready to go. Are you ready yet?"

"Well, I suppose I am ready," I answered as I quickly headed out of the bathroom. "I have water and some snacks for us. So, once my shoes are on…" Glancing down I noticed Leah's shoes were definitely on but on the wrong feet! Sighing I eased down to my knees again and started taking her sandals off.

"Mamma, what are you doing?" Leah shrieked. "I put my shoes on and now you are ruining them. They were perfect, Mamma. Stop!"

"Honey your shoes are on the wrong feet. I'm just trying to put them on correctly. Hold still please."

"No, Mamma, no! I look beautiful. I did a good job. Leave them alone!"

"Okay, okay. I won't touch them. Yes, you did a great job. Hopefully they won't make your feet hurt. Let's go then. Out the door!"

"Sheesh Mamma! Finally. I think we are going to be late." Flipping her hair over her shoulder she marched out the door.

CHAPTER 6

"Excuse me ma'am. Where are you going?"

Stopping just past the front desk at school, I turned and looked around. *Was she talking to me?* I wondered. Since no one else was around, I turned to look at the secretary and said politely, "I'm going to volunteer in my son's classroom. His teacher is expecting us."

"Well, you need to fill out this form, leave us your driver's license, and then wait until an escort from your son's class comes to get you. What is the teacher's name please?" Completely caught off guard, I simply just stared at the secretary. "Ma'am. The teacher? Her name?" Coming back to reality, I slowly turned toward the desk and offered Mrs. Thomas's name. The secretary quite efficiently grabbed her phone, punched in a pattern of numbers, and waited. "Yes, Mrs. …"

"Smith."

"…Smith is here. She says you are expecting her to volunteer in your classroom today. Yes, we will wait. Thank you." Turning to me she relayed the message she just received. "Mrs. Thomas is sending a couple students down to escort you to her classroom. Just fill out this form right quick and give me your license, and you will be ready when the students arrive."

"Sure. Um, is this procedure new or something? I don't remember this being mentioned during orientation."

"Yes, the Superintendent instituted this new procedure yesterday. You should be getting a letter in the mail today or tomorrow about it. It's just a safety precaution."

As I handed her my driver's license, I said, "I didn't know this campus was unsafe. Is there something I need to know?"

"No, Mrs. Smith. Everything is just fine. It's just a precaution." Just then Sam and another kid from his class walked into the office.

"Hi Mom! Mrs. Thomas sent us down here to pick you up. Follow us!" Suddenly I didn't feel very safe at all. As Leah and I started to follow Sam and his friend out of the office, the secretary called out, "Remember to stop back when you are done and get your license." She seemed entirely too happy.

***

Walking down the hallway toward Sam's classroom, muted noise wafted from each classroom we passed. Amid students' yelling, laughing, and whining and the teachers' voices raised giving instruction, came the familiar din of white noise associated with busy classrooms. Sam's classroom was at the very end of the hall, and as we approached, I saw a boy sitting at a desk outside the classroom door. "Why is there a boy sitting outside the classroom door," I asked Sam quietly?

"Oh, that's Walter. He has to sit outside the classroom a lot because he can't behave himself. That's what Mrs. Thomas says all the time. We are not supposed to talk to him, so don't say anything when we get to the door."

"That's sad," said Leah. I looked at Leah, squeezed her hand, and totally agreed with her sentiment. Ignoring Walter wasn't hard since as we passed by him on our way into the classroom, he didn't even look up from his empty desk. As my heart broke for him, we walked into Sam's classroom where my senses exploded.

"Mario, please for the last time, help Hannah pick up the reading corner. No! Don't lick her!! Oh Mario, never mind. Just go sit at your desk and put your head down. Hannah, come here. Betsy and Joe, would you mind finishing cleaning up the reading corner, so we can get started on our project? Hannah, you are fine. I know he licked you. It will be okay. Here, clean your face with this wipe. See? All better. Now, go sit down at your desk and wait for art."

Hannah, the licked victim, marched toward her desk but veered at the last second, stopped in front of Mario's desk, and blew raspberries in his face. Feeling vindicated, she whirled on her heel and plopped into her seat.

"Um, Mrs. Thomas?"

"Yes, Margaret."

"I don't feel very..." and with those final

words, Margaret lost her lunch and probably breakfast all over her desk and into the hair of the mortified girl in front of her. A painful silence erupted in the classroom as only a crisis can produce, and all eyes were either glued to Mrs. Thomas or vomiting Margaret. It was at this moment that I decided that Leah and I would come back another day.

Noticing our presence in the doorway for the first time, Mrs. Thomas said, "Class, this is Sam's mom and sister who have come to help us with our art project today; however, maybe we should postpone that until tomorrow?" Grateful she felt the same way, I told Leah to wait for me outside the classroom door – away from the chaos that had erupted from Margaret's upset stomach.

"Since there is only an hour left of the school day, I'm just going to take Sam home with me now if that is okay."

"That is just fine, Mrs. Smith. As you can see not much learning will happen before the bell rings."

Walking over to Sam, I quickly gathered up the papers on his desk while he went to retrieve his backpack from the hooks located outside the door to the outside access. "See you tomorrow, Mrs. Thomas." Quickly we were out the door leaving the mayhem behind. I no longer felt sorry for Walter as we passed him but happy that he hadn't been exposed to any germs that were released with Margaret's spewing. "Is it always like that Sam?"

"Not always. Today was definitely worse than some days. Thanks for taking me home. We wouldn't have done anything the rest of class anyway since the room would have had to be sanitized. Last week when Lydia puked, we all just sat at our desks with our heads down for like an hour while they cleaned up. The kids who had puke on them were sent to the nurse's office to get cleaned up. It was really gross."

"This has happened before?" I asked, mortified.

"Mom, I don't want someone to puke on me," stated Leah with her eyes wide with concern. She looked rather traumatized by the whole event. "I don't want to go to school if someone is going to throw up on me. You won't make me go, will you?"

"No one is going to puke on you honey." But even as I said it, my own confidence was really low. As we walked into the office the kids stayed close to me as I requested my ID back. "I'll also be checking out Sam Smith for the day. Our volunteering was cut short since Margaret, a girl in his class, just threw up, and it looks like the clean-up in his classroom might take a while."

"Here is your ID, Mrs. Smith, but I'm sorry you can't take Sam home with you. The school day is not finished."

Staring at the receptionist and trying to make sense of her rather bold statement, I simply looked at her and replied, "Well, I'm sorry but since he is my son, I will be taking him home whether the school day is finished or not." Having no intention of waiting for a response, I escorted my kids out the door.

CHAPTER 7

"Leah, I know you want to go to dance class today, but you have a fever. I know you don't want to get your whole class sick, especially Emily. I'm just hoping you will be well enough for pictures on Saturday. Oh, and we also get to pick up your costume on Saturday. I don't know about you, but I will be glad when this ballet class is over."

Cuddled up on the couch, covered in blankets, laying on her pillow and snuggling her stuffed bear, Leah croaked, "Fine. But you have to promise that we will go to pictures Mamma. I have to be beautiful for pictures, so everyone will like me."

"Oh, for Pete's sake. You are beautiful Leah, and you don't need some picture or performance to prove it. God made you just the way he wanted. Maybe you should take a nap, so you can get better."

Just as I was secretly hoping to lay down with her, my phone starting ringing and startled both of us.

"Hello?" I said.

"Mrs. Smith?"

"Yes, this is Mrs. Smith."

"This is Maria from Desert Elementary. Sam is in the nurse's office with a fever and needs to go home. Are you able to come pick him up?"

My heart had momentarily stopped beating with the receptionist's introduction, but now that I was breathing again and realizing that Sam's ailment was "just" a fever, I calmly replied, "Of course, I will be there shortly. Thank you. Bye."

"Who was that, Mamma?"

"It was the school, honey. Sam is sick, and we need to go pick him up. I'm sorry, but you have to come with me in the car. I'll carry you to the car, but you will have to put shoes on because we will have to walk to the office to pick up Sam. Do you think you can do it?"

"Oh poor Sam. Yes Mamma, I can go with you. If Sam feels yucky, he probably just wants to be home with us."

***

And so began the constant threat of illness. One kid's "allergies" were Sam's respiratory infections. Another kid's puking episodes from a simple "upset stomach" were Sam's flu bugs. As other kids recovered quickly and returned to school, Sam did not. And the moment the wheezing ceased and the constant coughing relented, another wave of illness would sweep through the school. Sam's inhaler was held hostage by the nurse Nazi which only exacerbated his coughing. His first semester of school dragged on, and as Thanksgiving approached, I spent more and more time asking God to protect Sam, to keep him healthy, but it seemed my prayers were going unanswered.

***

"Thanksgiving is in five days. What are you thinking we should do? Since the kids are sick, I really don't know if they will enjoy all the traditional food you make," said Matt.

"Well, I know I'm not up to it." Just then Sam's wracking cough could be heard from upstairs. "Leah is running a fever again, and it's all Sam can do to get through the next few days of school. I can't tell you how tired I am of arguing with that school nurse."

"Yeah, what was her reason again for not giving Sam his inhaler? It's so ridiculous that he can't keep it with him in the classroom."

"Oh, I'm so fed up with her. Every time I pick Sam up from school, I ask him if he coughed all day. He usually denies it because he knows it upsets me, but his friend, Peyton, has no problem detailing the agony he and the rest of the class endured with his coughing fits. He seems to constantly ask to go to the nurse's office to use his inhaler, and bless his teacher she lets him, but when he gets there the nurse insists that the only reason he would need his inhaler would be if his oxygen levels were low. His levels are always above 90% so his inhaler remains locked up in her drug locker. It's just idiocy that she won't let him have his inhaler in his desk. Claims it is "school policy" and that it is dangerous to the other kids in his classroom. If one of the kids in his classroom got a hold of his inhaler, it could harm him or her which is the most ridiculous reason I've ever heard. Perhaps those children should learn to keep their hands to themselves and not mess with things that don't belong to them! Well, I could care less about the rest of those germ-infested kids. They are the ones bringing in crap that Sam can't fight fast enough. If the little weasels in his class can't keep their cotton-pickin' hands out of his desk and off his inhaler, then they deserve what they get which in reality wouldn't be that bad. The inhaler won't hurt them. Sam's the only one who is being hurt with the school's policy. I'm at my wits end, Matt."

"Well hopefully a four-day weekend will bolster his strength to get through the last few weeks before Christmas break. Speaking of Christmas, when is Leah's "Nutcracker" performance scheduled again?"

"I am praying that he will stay well through Christmas, but right now I just think that is too much to ask. Leah's performance is the second Saturday in December, and I am so ready to be done with that cesspool of germs too. Anytime any child's tongue constantly licks green slime from their nose should be considered unfit to participate. I swear I am turning into a germaphobe!! I'm not signing her up for dance again in the spring. The program really isn't all that great anyway. It's glorified babysitting in a tutu. By the way her costume was $80.00, and do you know what her costume is? A tutu! Really, it should be made of gold," I sighed. "I'm sorry I just seem to be complaining about everything right now. I'm probably just tired. Being pregnant is harder this time, but that's no excuse to have a bad attitude."

"We're into the third trimester now, hon. You always feel better during the third trimester, so there's hope yet," replied Matt, poorly attempting to lighten the mood and make me feel better. "Maybe next week when you visit the new allergist and asthma doctor, he will have some good recommendations."

CHAPTER 8

"Looking through Sam's medical record, it looks like he's been chronically sick. I also see here that he was tested for allergies and Cystic Fibrosis when he was three. Is that correct?" asked Dr. Feldman.

"Yes, that is correct. He has struggled with illness since he was a baby," I responded.

"So, what are you looking for me to do for you?"

"Um, well our pediatrician referred us to you in hopes that if Sam's allergies could be controlled then perhaps his ability to fight infection would increase, and he wouldn't miss so much school." I tried to keep the irritation out of my voice, but I was sure my face conveyed my feelings without censure. I really wanted to ask him what he thought I was doing here? Did he think I just wanted to drive an hour and a half to be told there was nothing to be done for Sam? *If anyone's time was being wasted here, it was definitely mine!*

"I see. Well, based on his history – the

chronic illness, the asthma, the obvious allergies coupled with the current inhalers and all the allergy and asthma medication he's been taking since he was fifteen months old – I really only have two suggestions and one observation. Unfortunately, your family has moved to the worst place on the planet for allergy and asthma sufferers. That said, I am going to recommend you see an Ear, Nose and Throat Specialist to remove Sam's tonsils and adenoids, and I would like Sam to start a weekly regimen of allergy shots for three years. Does that sound reasonable?"

"Surgery and a three-year commitment to drive an hour and a half once a week for shots? I apologize for sounding flippant, but gee Doctor that sounds great. I can appreciate and understand the suggestion for removing his tonsils, but allergy shots for three years? What is the success rate?"

"Trust me, you are not the only mom to have that same reaction. Allergy shots are a huge commitment with a fantastic success rate in the patients it works for. I see you understand my vagueness. The only success rate I have is really just that simple and very unhelpful in making a decision. When allergy shots work, they work. But when they don't, well, at least you tried. Quite honestly if this was my kid, I would get his tonsils out at the end of the school year. We can start allergy shots now and then adjust accordingly for a couple weeks after his surgery. Really this is your last stop. If the allergy shots don't work, then he will just learn to manage better each year as he gets older, but it will not be easy. On the bright side, his immunity gets stronger and stronger each year and each time he's exposed at school. I'm sorry. You really did move to the worst place on the planet for asthma and allergy problems."

"Wow. Ok, so thank you for your honesty. I think Matt and I would like to pray about our decision, but if you could give us the name of the ENT and the allergy shot information to review, that would be great."

"Absolutely. I'll have the nurse bring in the ENT's contact information and paperwork for allergy shots. Whenever you make your decision, just give our office a call and we will schedule you for Sam's first round of allergy shots. It was good to meet you." Dr. Feldman shook my hand, and just like that he was gone.

***

"I don't know what to do Matt. Three years? So, every Wednesday after school all 4 of us schlep to the doctor for one shot that takes 2 seconds, but I learned today when I talked to the nurse that we would have to wait in the waiting room for 30 minutes after each shot to ensure no allergic reaction. Even though this might theoretically help Sam, I'm having a hard time justifying the time spent driving back and forth for our other kids."

"Well, I'm sure I could work something out with my schedule, so I could leave early on Wednesdays. Sam and I could just drive in at 4:00 or so and be home by dinner. You might have to take him on occasion, but I could as least help with this burden. So, the doctor really didn't have any great statistics to share to help us decide on whether this is worth it? Considering how often he is sick, I am inclined to get his tonsils out though. As for the allergy shots, I guess we could start them with the idea that we re-evaluate the success or failure in 6 months. Are you ok with just trying?"

"Dinner is ready kids! And don't forget to

wash your hands please," I shouted from the base of the stairs. "During my devotional this afternoon, I felt God telling me to try. I'm not sure if he was saying it was going to work. It just felt as if my heart wouldn't be at peace if we didn't try everything we could to help him feel better and succeed at school. I agree with getting his tonsils out and I feel as if we won't be able to unlock more answers until we see this allergy shot treatment through. It feels like an assignment to gain a greater understanding of what is to come. I truly have no idea what that means but I feel like we need to follow this through in order to find our path forward."

"Smells awesome, Mom! Mac-n-cheese, my favorite. So, are we celebrating something?" Sam asked.

"Not exactly," Matt replied. Adding a cheeky smile he said, "But hopefully it will make you feel a bit better about what the doctor has planned for you!"

"Somehow that doesn't sound like a good thing, Dad. Mom, what's going on?" Sam asked.

"Let's say the blessing, and then I'll answer your question. Dear Lord, thank you for your bountiful blessings. Thank you for your continued faithfulness and protection. Thank you for guiding our decisions and giving us peace when our minds are troubled. We ask you for continued strength in the months ahead. We ask that you nourish our bodies with the blessing of food provided tonight. It's in Jesus' name we pray, Amen."

Not wasting anytime breaking the news to Sam, I said, "Remember during the doctor visit today, Dr. Feldman shared that he feels like it is in your best interests to get your tonsils and adenoids out and start weekly allergy shots? Well, your dad and I have talked about it. We think that having your tonsils and adenoids out is a good idea and we feel like we should give the allergy shots a try."

"Oh, Mark, a kid in my class, got his tonsils out last summer, and he said that he got to eat ice cream every day! Can I have ice cream every day?" Sam asked excitedly.

"Well, I suppose if it helps, then... yeah. So, you're okay with this idea?" Matt asked.

Through a mouthful of food, Sam replied, "Well, yeah. Mark said it was no big deal."

"I don't know if I'd say it's no big deal, but I know you can handle it. So, what do you think about getting allergy shots?"

Sam paused and then replied, "Well, getting shots isn't high on my fun list, but I'm willing to try it if it might make me feel better. I think my coughing annoys the kids in the classroom, but I really can't stop. Maybe the kids will like me better if I stop coughing. What do you think Mom?"

With my heart in my stomach, I looked at Sam and said, "Maybe you just need new friends. We love you coughing or no coughing. Well, it's decided then. I'll call the doctor tomorrow."

And winter turned into spring …

CHAPTER 9

"I know you are tired, Sam. There's only 4 more weeks of school left, and then we are done for the summer," I encouraged Sam, even though I felt like crawling back to bed myself. Since Grace was born, school became even harder. No one was looking forward to the end of the school year more than me.

"Is Grace up yet, Mamma?" asked Leah.

"Not yet." Yawning, I continued, "She was up at 3:30 this morning, so she will be due to eat again soon. I'm hoping to get Sam dropped off before I have to feed her, but we will see. Do you think you could try and keep her distracted in the car on the way to school if I wake her just before we leave?"

"Oh yes, Mamma, I love to try and make her smile."

Excellent, I thought to myself. This early school drop off followed by a 45-minute nursing session in the car in the school parking lot was getting old. Our air conditioning in the car couldn't keep up in the Arizona heat, which made the experience all the more unpleasant. Adding more misery were the weekly PTA meetings before lunch which just messed up Grace's nap schedule.

What is wrong with me? I thought to myself. *Where is the super mom I intended to be at the start of the school year? Who cares if Grace's nap schedule gets messed up? Other mom's do it and don't seem to care about the lack of any schedule for their kids. Why couldn't I not care?*

And then there was the whole volunteering thing. I was so excited to help in the classroom; so excited to be the best room mom ever; so excited to just be involved. At first Sam's teacher needed a lot of volunteer help, and with just Leah, it was easy because the teacher allowed her to participate in the activities. But as the school year has worn on, the teacher has needed and wanted me less and less.

I guess it's a good thing considering schlepping both girls into the classroom was becoming a real chore, not to mention a distraction for the other kids. Ugh, especially when that snotty-nosed Peter kept playing with Grace's hands and touching her face and kissing her nose!

"Mom!" yelled Sam.

"Good grief, Sam, what?"

"Sorry Mom but I've been trying to get your attention. You've kinda been in a trance. Don't you hear Grace? She's been wailing for a few minutes now."

"Oh sorry honey, I was just thinking, and what time is… Sam!, Leah! Hurry! We have to leave now! I'll get Grace, and I'll meet you two in the car. No time to feed her now."

Beaming, Leah looked at me and said, "Oh that's ok Mamma. I know just how to make her happy." And so, the race continued.

***

Sitting outside of our favorite coffee shop under a shade umbrella, Sally and I talked while the kids enjoyed an iced Frappuccino.

"Oh, Sally, I just don't know what to

do. This whole school thing is just not what I expected. I feel like I have no idea what is going on in the classroom, and I certainly don't feel like I am a part of my child's education. Maybe I'm not supposed to be involved. Maybe my only role is to drop my kid off, pick my kid up, and do only what the teacher says. Don't even get me started on how disruptive the school schedule is for Leah and Grace. All I say anymore is 'hurry up we gotta go,' or 'hurry up we're going to be late,' or 'sorry I had to wake you up but we have to pick up Sam.' I guess I'm just complaining. I mean, did I really expect that I would be able to retain a schedule once school started?"

Sally looked at me over the rim of her sunglasses and said, "We are talking about you: the queen of schedules and order. I think you are just going to have to get over yourself. I know it's hard, but what other choice is there?" Tapping her finger to her chin, Sally exclaimed with a twinkle in her eye, "Oh, I know! You could homeschool! Or there is always the bus."

"Well honestly you are not the first person to suggest the bus, but I don't know. It just doesn't feel right. And I have been praying about homeschooling, but I just don't know about that either. What if I screw my kids up? Or worse, what if the state thinks I'm screwing my kids up and takes them away from me? You hear stories about that you know."

"Well as I have always told you, homeschooling is a calling. If God calls you, he will equip you and protect you."

"My brain seems to know that, but my heart doesn't believe it yet. I'm sure there is something I can do to make Sam's school year better next year, right? Maybe his teacher will be more open to him keeping his inhaler in his desk, and since this will be his second year of school, maybe he won't get sick as often? Grace will be older too, so that means less interruption of her many feeding schedules. I know I won't be able to help out in the classroom, but I can still participate in classroom parties and activities. I'm sure next year will be better," I stated quite matter-of-factly.

"Maybe you are right," Sally replied dripping sarcasm.

CHAPTER 10

"Hi buddy! How was your day? One week to go!"

"MOM! You'll never believe what happened!"

"Oh my gosh, Sam, are you ok? Is anyone hurt?"

"No Mom," Sam groaned. "Everyone is fine. Well, maybe not the aliens."

"What aliens?" Leah asked excitedly.

"Yeah, what aliens," I snickered.

Ignoring my sarcasm, Sam continued, "You know that Peyton hung out with his mom after school yesterday, right? Well, he told me that at about 2:30 p.m. yesterday afternoon the principal locked the school down because aliens landed! Oh man I'm so bummed that I missed it, Mom. I could have seen an alien!"

Whipping her head from side to side and struggling in her car seat to see out the back window of the car, Leah wondered excitedly,

"Oh where did Peyton say they landed? Was it where we buy gas? Oh! I bet they landed at the McDonalds because they were probably hungry."

Deciding to get to the bottom of Sam's story, I did a U-turn into a parking spot in the school lot and put the vehicle in park. Then I turned around and looked at Sam. His eyes were just sparkling, and he looked a little crazed. I hated to tell him what really happened.

"Look Sam, aliens did not land yesterday."

"Did too, Mom. Peyton wouldn't lie about something as important as this."

"Oh I know that he is not lying, but it's not what you guys think it is. Remember how all year Mrs. Thomas has practiced with you guys about what to do in case the school has to lock its doors so that no one can come in and no one can go out? Well, that is what happened yesterday. I got a letter in the mail today from the superintendent describing what happened yesterday afternoon after all the buses had left for the day."

"Did the super guy describe what the aliens looked like Mamma?" Leah asked, eyes shining. "I wonder where their spaceship is. I wonder if it is still there! Maybe we can go see it, Mamma!"

Trying really hard to remain serious, I replied, "Well they didn't have a spaceship, so we definitely can't go see it."

"Bummer!" Sam exclaimed from the backseat. He gave Leah a reassuring look that suggested they could see it next time.

"And the superintendent did kind of describe what the aliens looked like. But before I go any further, I need to clarify something with you."

"We know Mom. We are not supposed to talk to strangers, and I'm pretty sure that aliens fit into the stranger danger category. But it would have been so cool to see them!"

"You're right Sam. You shouldn't talk to strangers, but aliens don't look much different from you or I."

"WHAT???" Sam asked, eyes wide with concern. "You mean there are aliens living among us now, and we wouldn't know because they look just like us?"

"Sam! Maybe you have one in your class!" Leah exclaimed.

Chuckling out loud I looked Sam in the eyes, "Sam. There are no such things as aliens. What Peyton is talking about and what the superintendent wrote to all the parents about was an incident that happened yesterday with illegal aliens."

Awestruck, Sam whispered, "Illegal aliens." Then remembering I said aliens didn't exist, Sam squinted his eyes and answered with a bit of frustration in his tone, "But Mom you just said that aliens don't exist."

Sighing, I said, "You are right. There are no such things as little green aliens from outer space. There are such things as illegal aliens."

"Well then where do these 'illegal aliens' come from, Mom, if not from outer space?" Sam snorted looking at Leah as if his logic was obvious.

"Mexico. At least the ones from yesterday"

"So, Mexico has aliens too?" Sam asked with

a look of shock on his face. "I wonder if they are all over the world."

"Ok, let's start over. Aliens don't exist. Illegal aliens do exist. Green men from outer space do not exist. Illegal aliens from Mexico do exist. Yes, illegal aliens could possibly be worldwide."

"This is so confusing!" Leah exclaimed slapping her hand to her forehead.

"I know sweetheart. But listen, illegal aliens are simply people who come into our country, or any country really, without permission from our government or the government of the country they are entering. The people yesterday were from Mexico, and they had entered our country without permission. Apparently, they were driving dangerously fast. So, the police contacted the school and told them to lock it down, so no one would get hurt. The men were dangerous because they also had guns and drugs in their car. But the police arrested them so now everyone is safe."

"Mamma?" Leah whispered from the back seat. "We have drugs too. Are the police going to come find us because they think we are dangerous?"

"Oh no, no, no honey. We have prescription drugs that have been given to us by a doctor for your asthma. The drugs that these men had were very harmful drugs not from doctors. The police don't need to find us."

"So, aliens didn't land." Sam announced irritably. "All that excitement for nothing. Well, I just hope that the 'illegal aliens' don't come back since that just caused a bunch of confusion. I wonder if Peyton knows they weren't from space. Well, I'm not telling him because he won't believe me. I'll let his mother tell him the bad news."

Trying hard not to laugh, I responded, "Well I'm sure Peyton's mom will let him know who the 'illegal aliens' really are and where they are from." Trying to effectively change the subject, I remarked, "All this talk of McDonalds has made me want some ice cream. Who's game?"

"Really?"

"Awesome!" Leah and Sam high-fived in the back. Leaning over so Leah could hear him, Sam conspired, "The illegal aliens must have really upset Mom. We never get ice cream right after school. Let's make sure we tell Dad when he gets home. This might upset him too. Who knows, maybe he will feel like he needs ice cream and will make a milkshake for us. That's two ice cream treats in one day. Score!"

"Deal," Leah agreed.

Hearing their exchange from the back seat made me giggle. *Aliens landing!* I thought to myself. *How silly.* Then it hit me. *Aliens landing!!!!* Every parent's nightmare had happened yesterday after all the children were safe on the bus or at home. The dreaded words... LOCKDOWN. *Dear Jesus please keep my child safe at school. Please keep all the children and all the teachers and staff safe at school. Wrap your arms around the school buildings and protect everyone who is inside. Protect them as the teachers teach and the students learn. Please Jesus, I don't want another lockdown letter from the superintendent. Please Jesus, I beg you.*

Suddenly I was no longer in the mood for ice cream.

CHAPTER 11

"Let's go you all!! We don't want to miss Sam's graduation ceremony."

"This is sort of ridiculous don't you think?" Matt commented under his breath.

"Yeah, just a little, but all the schools are doing this now so there's no escaping it."

Rolling his eyes Matt whispered in my ear, "Well we could just skip it and go find something fun to do instead."

"Stop it," I laughed. "It's a big deal to Sam that we all go. So, figure out a way to enjoy yourself."

"I will. Even though I think it's ridiculous. It's just kindergarten!"

I turned and gave him my best 'mom' look. "Ok! Ok! I'll behave. I promise."

The parking lot at the school was packed so we had to park across the street at the grocery store. Leah thought it was just another adventure which I suppose was a good thing since she wasn't complaining. Grace was not pleased however, to be buckled into her stroller. The clear blue sky made the blazing 103-degree temperature even more horrendous, and as we burst through the school office doors, I think we all audibly exhaled sighs of relief.

"Hi. We are here for the kindergarten graduation."

"Name of the graduate, please."

"Sam Smith."

"Thank you. I'll need both your driver's licenses, please."

Handing over our driver's licenses I asked, "Do we need to wait for an escort?"

"No, not today Mrs. Smith. The district has decided that holding all driver's licenses should be enough security. You may head to Sam's classroom. Just remember to stop back here after the party to pick them up."

"Thank you. We will."

Back out in the heat, Matt retorted, "Duh.

Like I'd forget to get my license on the way out. There has got to be a better way than filing all those licenses for every visitor. What a nightmare for the office. I'm not sure I understand what it is they think they are preventing. I thought we used to be able to just go to Sam's classroom. What happened and why did they change it?"

"Don't you remember when I told you I came to volunteer a few weeks after school had started and the rules had changed? It's made everyone so stiff and unfriendly – as if they are afraid to get too personal."

As we rounded the hallway the din of voices roared from each of the classrooms.

"Look Mamma! There is Sam's class." Leah took off running toward the classroom.

"Well, someone is excited to see Sam graduate today."

Just as I finished my sentence Sam peeked his head out of the classroom door and motioned for me to hurry. Leaving the stroller with Matt I rushed toward Sam.

Breathless and flustered he announced,

"Mom, my cap won't stay on. I've tried everything." Handing me his cap he looked at Matt, "Hi Dad."

Trying to deflect his obvious tension, I beamed, "Don't you look handsome! Well, I just so happen to know exactly how to fix that problem." Digging into my purse I triumphantly retrieved the solution. Winking and cradling Sam's face in my hands, I whispered, "Bobby Pins fix everything." Working my magic, the hat was soon secured to his head. "There, just don't go banging your head around like you are a rock star and it should stay in place."

Beaming, Sam exclaimed, "Thanks Mom! You guys better find a place to sit. We are about to get started."

Matt looked around the room. "So, the ceremony is going to take place in here?"

Surprised he was even asking that question I responded, "Well of course. Where did you think we would be?"

"But where are we supposed to sit?"

"It looks like she has all the chairs for the

parents along the back wall. How cute is this?"

"Not really very cute at all. Those chairs are kid chairs. We're expected to sit in miniature chairs?"

"Oh honestly Matt. What did you think we were going to sit on? Of course, the miniature chairs. We are in a kindergarten class. Nothing in here is big. I think I'll take Grace out of the stroller and park it in the hallway since it is so crowded in here. I'll just hold her on my lap."

Handing Grace to Matt, I quickly drove the stroller through the class and parked it just outside the classroom door, and then returned to find Matt still confused about the seating arrangements.

On the verge of hysteria Matt exclaimed, "I think we have fallen through the rabbit hole in *Alice in Wonderland*. If I sit down, I'm going to break something. I seriously don't even know how THAT guy is sitting down. Oh my gosh! Maybe the chair is totally broken beneath him and he is too embarrassed to stand up." Clearly distraught, Matt looked at me and pointed to the door to the outside located just behind and a little to the left of the row of audience seating. "I think I'll stand."

Tilting my head and looking at THAT guy I tried not to snicker. "You're right. Although you are by no means as wide as him, I see your point. The girls and I are going to sit though. So, if you are going to stand then you can take pictures considering you have the best vantage point." I smugly smiled at Matt over my shoulder as we headed toward our seats.

"That is one good looking diploma you've got there Sam. Your mom and I are so proud of you. I see here the class voted you 'Best Dressed.' Not sure how they figured that since everyone has the same uniform."

"Matt!"

"What? It's true, isn't it?" Matt laughed, eyes twinkling.

"Sam, ignore your father. He's just cranky because he had to stand still for a whole 30 minutes."

Ruffling Sam's hair, Matt said, "Joking aside,

you did great son. We love you very much."

"Thanks Dad."

"Well, I never want to attend another one of these ceremonies again. Talk about BORING! And the treats were so lame!" Leah exclaimed with her hands on her hips as she rolled her eyes.

"So, you are planning on skipping your graduation ceremony?" Matt asked.

"No." Leah stated. "But I think we can have a better ceremony and party at home."

"Well, I agree that the food was lame and we could totally do better at home. But since we are out, who is in the mood for ice cream?" Matt asked excitedly.

"I AM!" Sam and Leah shouted together.

And spring turned into summer.

Chapter 12

"But why can't I start school Mamma? I want to learn with the big kids."

"I know you do sweetheart, but the rules won't allow children to start school until they are five years old."

"Well, that's stupid. I bet I'm just as smart as most of those kids Mamma."

Chuckling I answered, "I have no doubt you are sweet pea. But I really don't want you to be gone all day like Sam is. I miss him when he is at school. I know, maybe we can talk to Emily's mom and see what she thinks you and I could do together at home this year. We don't have to spend a lot of money to do our own school. It could be fun, just you and me. How does that sound?"

Eyes wide with excitement, Leah agreed, "That is a great idea Mamma!! I'll do school just like Sam, but my teacher will be so much better than his. I'm going to go tell him now." And off she ran with teddy in hand to share the good news with Sam.

Smiling I looked down at the journal entry I had been writing prior to Leah's public protest about the school age requirement and continued to pour my heart into the worn pages.

School. Just two weeks away. How is that possible? Sam's surgery went well for the most part and the allergy shots have weirdly become our weekly norm. He doesn't even flinch when the needle goes in anymore. He says he doesn't feel it. I'm so amazed at this kid. He has taken every suggestion from the doctors and followed through with them without complaints. I really don't know if the allergy shots are even working. Between surgery and sickness this summer he's really only had a couple weeks where he felt good. At least he wasn't sick when we visited Nana and Papa in Colorado. It was so nice to just relax, enjoy the weather and let the kids play outside without fear.

Fear. Growing up I don't ever remember being afraid to play outside. Of course, there was stranger danger and all that but never fear of playing outside. Reactions to fear are divided here. Precaution is either a natural companion or there is none at all. I guess like most things people either tend to be aware or nonplussed. I never expected to live in a town where the threat of human trafficking was real. I can still remember the day when a mom I had just met warned me to keep an eye on my kids because they could be worth a lot of money. At the time I wasn't sure if she was kidding or serious. I know being extra careful and alert seems silly to most, but better safe than sorry, right?

"Tonka" tracks. That's what our neighbor calls them. I guess the illegal traffic has gotten worse over the last five years. Apparently when our community was built it was free of "tonka tracks." Now, helicopters fly over the house constantly. At first, I just thought they were news copters and thought they were very thorough and accurate about their traffic reports. Eventually I started to recognize them as belonging to the Border Patrol. I never thought I would live somewhere that my kids couldn't ride their bikes around the block, play outside unattended, or even walk to a friend's house alone. It's monotonously flat here so bike riding is brilliantly easy, but fear cripples my momma's heart. Since all our kids have blond hair and blue eyes, they are highly valuable in the trafficking market, or at least that's what people say. It's hard to ignore what people

say.

And now school is starting and the superintendent is sending out letters about all the added security and how we should be preparing our kids at home in the event of a lockdown. I'm seriously in another dimension. In what world did I ever think that public school was not safe? In what world did I ever think that my kids couldn't play outside for fear of being taken. In what world did I ever think of how I could avoid sending my kids to school? But what choice is there really? Honestly, I have no idea. I keep hearing all of these alternative school choices but it just seems so not normal. But who coined the definition of normal to begin with? Maybe alternative schooling is just as normal as public schooling. So, if public school doesn't work, there is private school, charter school, university model style school, K-12 online school, STEM school, and of course the proverbial homeschool. I guess I need to just pray more and wait for answers. Honestly, I don't even know what to pray for right now.

I put the pen down, closed my eyes and breathed deep. Quietly I prayed, "Please God just show me the way you want me to go.

Even amidst all the choices I feel like I'm running out of options."

Chapter 13

Summer is never long enough, I thought as I hit the snooze button for the third time. *The first day of Sam's 1st grade year. Yippee. Oh my goodness when did my excitement of last year turn into sarcasm this year? Ok, Kit. Knock it off. Get up! This is Sam's first day of 1st grade. He has a good teacher, the sun is shining, and he is well. It's going to be a good year. My goodness why am I so tired?*

As I got dressed, I tried to improve my attitude and by the time I arrived in the kitchen for breakfast and lunch preparations, I managed to at least look excited for the first day of school.

This year will be different, I'm sure. Didn't the doctor warn us that he would miss at least half of his kindergarten year due to illness? And hasn't he missed about that? Yes, he did. So, now it's rainbows and unicorns from here. It can only get better, I reassured myself.

I started to hit my rhythm. As I set the spinach and meat frying to make eggs for breakfast, I grabbed for the gluten free bread out of the fridge. Just as I added the eggs to the pan, Grace started crying upstairs.

"And so the race begins," I sighed as I turned off the stove and headed up the stairs.

"Well, good morning handsome," I greeted Sam as he met me coming out of Grace's room with her seated comfortably on my hip. "Did you sleep well? Are you excited for your first day?"

Skipping down the hall and meeting us in front of Grace's room, Leah smiled, "Good morning Mamma!! I slept good, Mamma. I'm really excited about OUR first day of school together. See, Mamma? I'm all dressed just like Sam so we can start school when we get home."

"You totally interrupted me, Leah. Mom asked me first. Geez, you can be so rude!" And with that Sam stomped off down the stairs.

"Well, someone is grumpy this morning. However, Leah you should not have interrupted. You should apologize when we get downstairs."

"Ok Mamma. Sorry. Why isn't Sam excited this morning?"

"I'm not sure honey. Let's go find out."

Leah grabbed my hand and we walked downstairs into the kitchen. Sam sat slumped in his chair at the table facing the stairs.

Leah, Grace, and I hadn't hit the bottom of the stairs yet before he blurted, "I don't want to go to school. I want to stay home with you guys. The school nurse won't let me have my medicine, I'll probably hate my teacher, and recess stinks."

Descending the last few steps, placing Grace on the floor with some toys, I quietly sat down next to Sam. Kissing the top of his head I breathed in the smell of him. Swallowing mounting tears I said, "Oh Sam. We don't want you to go either, but you have to. I'm sure the school nurse will be better this year and you liked your teacher when you met her at back-to-school night. Peyton is also in your class this year so that is really exciting. I know recess is not your favorite, but I've been praying that the kids will be nicer this year. You have to give it a chance. You just can't judge the year before you have started it."

Throwing his arms around my neck, with tears streaming down his face, I seriously almost lost it. All I wanted to do was hold onto my boy. My boy that still smells like a baby at times and like sweat and dirt at others. My boy who had been so brave this past year and so excited about school, but now so distraught. My sweet, smart, amazing, loving boy. *Please God, guide my words to help him*, I prayed. Pulling his face to meet mine and wiping his tears I could see the resignation in his eyes.

"I'm ok now Mom. I should probably eat since we have to leave soon. May I have peanut butter and jelly for lunch? I'm sorry I got so upset. And I'm sorry I yelled at you too, Leah. I'll try to have a good year Mom. I promise. I'll ask God to help me have a good year."

Leah chimed in, "That's a great idea Sam! God can fix anything. Right, Mamma? Oh, and I'm sorry for interrupting you."

"I love you so much, Sam. You will be great this year." Kissing his check and turning to Leah I said, "And you are so very smart, Leah. God can fix anything. We'd better hurry though, so let's eat!!

***

"I thought you said we were going to start school today Mamma," Leah asked as we rang the doorbell at Sally's house.

"Well, we are, kind of. Emily's mom invited us over to look at her school stuff so we can see what some of it looks like so we can decide if we really need all the books or if we are just going to do our own thing. Plus Ms. Sally was just so excited when I told her that I was going to do some school at home with you this year that I couldn't say no when she invited us over to share what she has."

Opening the door with her usual southern charm, Sally joyfully greeted us. "Well, hi guys!" Come on in. Please excuse the mess. Emily has been determined this morning to drag all her school out at once instead of one subject at a time. She wants Leah to see all she has to do for school today. Additionally, I've brought some boxes in from the garage that have Emily's school from last year."

"Thank you so much for letting us come over and look through your stuff, especially during your school day. I have to admit, I'm a little intimidated with this whole idea. I mean, why do school at home when there are accredited pre-schools? Who says I'm qualified to provide Leah with what she needs? What if I totally ruin her? I'm sorry, Sally. That sounded really rude and disrespectful. I didn't mean it that way. I just truly have no clue what "homeschooling" looks like."

Handing me a cup of coffee Sally replied, "I totally get it and no offense taken. This "homeschooling" thing does sound a little hokey. But I can honestly promise you that you can't screw up pre-school." Curling her feet up on her couch Sally continued, "Now it's a little pricey if you were to order the whole pre-school package but the way I looked at it when I started is that I would be spending at least double that amount by sending Emily to an accredited pre-school. Plus, I wouldn't get to see or be a part of her milestones. I know you think that you aren't supposed to witness your children's milestones because that is how society raised us to think. If we feel bad that we missed seeing our child write their name for the first time or read their first sentence or discover that eggs float in salt water, then we are told to get over it. It's time to let go. Quit being a helicopter mom. I've never been one for sticking to conventions so for me it was easy to buck the system. Seeing your child sound out words day after day and struggling as all early learners do to understand their native language and then see the light of understanding shine out from their eyes when they do get it, is just, well... priceless. That sounds super cheesy but when that happened with Emily after we had been struggling for what seemed forever; I knew I could never let someone else take my firsts from me."

"Mamma, do you see all the books they have? We have some of the very same books! Someday I want to read all the books ever written just to know what they could possibly have to say! That would be a lot of books wouldn't it Mamma? Like, like a gazillion!"

Chuckling at Leah's enthusiasm, I said, "Well I suppose that would take a lifetime. Why don't you go check out what other books they have?"

"Can I? Thanks Mamma!!"

"Well, that will keep her occupied for a while. She just loves to look at the book jackets and pictures inside the books, if there are any, and just create the stories in her head. I think sitting next to her and helping her read her very first words would be pretty amazing. I was getting a little weepy as you were describing it. But is it really like that? I know that I've missed a lot of Sam's firsts, but I've never really realized how many firsts I have missed, and honestly, I didn't know that there were even firsts to begin with until sitting here with you. Knowing that I've missed a lot of his firsts makes me sad, especially considering that I figured I was just supposed to miss them. That's something I will have to think about some more since I've never heard anyone put it the way you just did. I guess from a societal perspective preschool should be structured and predictable, loud and sociable. Is that what your day looked like with Emily? David, your youngest, wasn't born yet when you started pre-school with Emily, correct?"

"Correct. I was just pregnant with David so it wasn't until we started kindergarten that I had to balance a newborn with school. Again, you need to remember that Leah is only 4. Her attention span won't include a full day of structured and predictable activities. And I know you. You don't have loud, screaming kids, and they have no problem being social. Leah is in dance with Emily and she has friends in her Sunday school class at church. She and Sam play together when he gets home from school and now that you have Grace, Leah helps you by playing the little mommy. I don't think you need to worry about the social aspect of pre-school. Your kids are plenty socialized."

"But isn't preschool where they supposedly start to learn to live within structured boundaries? With school and with other kids?"

"Ah, now I understand your concern. Yes, preschool begins to teach kids that there are 'times' for everything. A time for play, a time for listening, a time for work, a time for snack, a time for rest. But it should also be a time of fun exploring and learning through doing. I wanted to be a part of all their times. I didn't want to give up the time I had with them until it WAS time. Learning at home is just so much fun and special. Plus, field trips are a great treat too. It gets you out of the house and it counts for schoolwork as well. Please don't think that once you homeschool Leah for preschool that you can't enroll her in public school when she's ready for kindergarten or whatever age you would want to transition her to public school if at all. I've known families that have homeschooled and public schooled their children on and off through the years depending on the needs of the family and the child. I personally don't think that is a great idea but it's an option. You are in control of your child's education which is really freeing."

"Ok, so now that my mind is whirling, show me the stuff. Show me ALL the stuff and then tell me what I really don't need since you've done this before. Never in a million years would I have thought I would be sitting looking through preschool homeschool curriculum. Honestly the first time you mentioned you homeschooled I thought you might be a little weird. Now look at me sitting here with you discussing homeschool. I'm sorry Sally, for judging you that way."

"Don't feel bad. You are not the first to have judged homeschool or me. God had a plan bringing us together and I am so glad He did. However, I will tell you homeschooling is not always easy or pretty, and I still truly believe that homeschooling is a calling not to be taken lightly. However, in my opinion, it is the greatest calling you can receive."

Chapter 14

"She dubbed it 'a calling,' Matt. I don't even know what to do with that. I mean, what if I actually decide to homeschool but God never calls me? Can I do it anyway? Or can I only do it if called? And if I am called, what in the world is He thinking?"

"Well, Sally must have said a lot of stuff to set your mind twirling in the homeschool direction. Remember darlin', God does not call the equipped. He equips the called."

"I know that, but seriously. Does God know who he would be calling? Don't you remember Matt? Teachers did not think of me when the word academics came to mind. I was voted best dressed, not most likely to grow up and teach!! And let's not forget that my math teacher called me stupid in front of the whole class, and I was discouraged from taking all AP classes in high school except English. Apparently, the teachers thought I was versed at communicating but nothing else. Good grief, Matt, I got a "D" in my experimental math class in college for pity's sake. I am not the teacher of the family. My sister is the born teacher. I'm not actually sure what I was born to do but all the educators in my life silently and unanimously voted me 'most likely to not TEACH!"

Panic reaching a whole new level in my brain, Matt quietly reached out and pulled me to him. "First, the teacher who called you stupid should have been fired. Second, you were educated by a system, not by people who cared about you or saw your potential. You my dear, got a bad deal from our grand education system. However, true to your personality, you succeeded on your own. Don't forget you graduated summa cum laude from college. You are the smartest person I know. In fact, I think God would be crazy not to call you. That said, it's a huge decision to homeschool and should not be taken lightly but at the moment I thought we were only considering homeschooling Leah in preschool. And if we did decide to homeschool preschool, I mean, it is preschool. Doesn't that seem pretty doable? How can you screw up preschool?"

Having lost all control of my tears, I mumbled into Matt's chest, "Well, you haven't seen what I can do yet. Apparently, it's a pretty big deal. I'm behind the times Matt. In just a few short years from when Sam went to preschool until now, there are interviews that happen. Yeah, I should have made my interview list well before now because now parents are getting their acceptance letters in the mail. It's too late to interview preschools. Who knew that education became competitive at preschool? My goodness Matt, she is only 4. She loves to color and build with Legos, and dig in the garden. She's so determined to do anything Sam does. She even taught herself to ride her bike without training wheels in the back yard. Remember? How can I send her away to have her firsts without me?" And with that the tears started again. "I'm sorry, I don't know what is wrong me. I've been so tired lately and apparently exceptionally emotional. Maybe it's… OOOOH MATT!"

Shock and concern wrinkling his forehead, Matt asked, "What baby, what is it? It's going to be ok, really. Whatever God tells us to do, we will do."

Pale now and staring into Matt's eyes, I announced, "I'm pregnant. I haven't taken a test but I just know. You know? Oh, wow, life is going to get stupid crazy now. Matt. Matt!!"

"Another baby!" Standing up and fist bumping the air Matt 'wahooed,' lifted me up and kissed me. "Another baby! God is good honey. All the time He is good."

That night in bed as I made my lists in my head, I handed my worries to God. *Dear heavenly Father, thank you for the blessing of another child. I pray for my health and the health of the new life forming in me. Lord, I also lift up my worries and concerns and hurts tonight. Help Matt and I to discern what is right for our family. Lead us in deciding where Leah should attend preschool, and if homeschooling is your will for us. We trust that you will lead us in a direction that fulfills your will for our lives and the lives of our children. I love you Lord. It's in Jesus' name that I pray, Amen.*

***

"Mamma, I'm done with writing the alphabet. And I've written my name, my whole name a hundred times!! When can we do something else Mamma?"

Looking over at Leah's paper where a crooked row of letters and the name Leah Smith was written a whopping 5 times I responded, "Give me a minute honey. I need to switch the laundry over to the dryer. The doctor said we have to change sheets every few days for allergies and I'm a little late this week. And then I need to feed Grace."

"You just said 'in a minute.' How long is a minute anyway, Mamma? It must be a really long time. And you just fed Grace. How often do you need to feed her anyway?"

"Leah Smith. Don't you sass me. I'm only one person doing the job of fifty. I printed out some number sheets after I finished the dishes this morning. Why don't you work on those while I feed Grace? You know better than to ask me how often she eats. Do you want someone to get annoyed every time you want a snack?"

Leah stared at me with her big old blue eyes and shook her head remorsefully. "I didn't think so. Now you go on and practice your numbers. I'm doing the best I can. Remember what your dad and I told you? We are not buying a formal curriculum until we've heard definitively from God that he wants us to homeschool. So, for now we have the book we bought at Costco and whatever pages I can print out. When Grace goes down for her afternoon nap you and I will read some books. Ok?"

"Ok Mamma. I'm sorry."

"It's ok sweetheart. I'm awful proud of you for enjoying learning so much. We'll figure out what we are supposed to do. Don't you worry."

As I turned toward the laundry room the kitchen phone rang. "Oh, for Pete's sake, who is that? I am busy right now!"

"Hello?" I answered with a slight irritation in my voice.

"Mrs. Smith?"

"Speaking."

"Hi, Mrs. Smith, my name is Vera Sparks. You reached out to me several months ago regarding preschool for your daughter, Leah? Well, I wanted to touch base with you to see if you were still interested in my preschool program. I just had a cancellation, so I have one space available for your daughter if you want it."

Stunned, I stared blankly into the laundry room.

"Mrs. Smith? Are you there?"

"Oh, um. Sorry. Yes, I'm here. I'm so sorry. You caught me completely off guard. To be perfectly honest preschool had totally fallen off my radar because I didn't think there were any openings left anywhere. Leah was just sitting down to work in a workbook I bought her at Costco."

"That's wonderful. Those are definitely great resources. Well, I understand how I could have caught you off guard. We haven't spoken in several months. But since I told you I would put you on my waiting list, I wanted to make sure I extended the offer to you first. Would you still be interested?"

"I, um, wow! Well, I'm actually not sure. Am I allowed to talk to my husband?"

Chucking, Vera replied, "Yes. You are definitely allowed to talk to your husband. In fact, I would suggest it. Please speak with your husband tonight. Let's see, today is Wednesday, so how about Friday? Can you get back to me by Friday?"

"Yes. Yes, I can. Thank you so much. Ok, so I'll talk to you soon. Thanks again!"

"Until Friday, then. Bye."

"Who was that Mamma?"

"That was Ms. Sparks, a preschool teacher. I talked to her several months ago about you attending her preschool class. She has just had a student cancel so she is wondering if you want to go."

"Oh," Leah quietly sighed as she looked down and suddenly became very interested in the kitchen table.

"Leah?"

"Yes, Mamma?"

"What is the matter?"

"Nothin'."

"Leah Smith, I know you better than that. Now you tell me what is going on in that head of yours."

"But Mamma, I don't want to hurt your feelings. Didn't you tell me that if I couldn't say something nice then to not say anything at all?"

Trying not to smile, "Yes, Leah, that's right. But I am asking you to speak your mind. I'll be ok, I promise."

"Really? You really promise? Pinky swear?"

"Pinky swear." Turning to face my general direction and swinging her legs distractedly, Leah blurted, "Oh Mamma, I know I said that doing school at home would be so fun, and it is! Except when you have to do the laundry and feed Grace and make dinner and pick up the clutter, whatever that means," she murmured under her breath. "And once the new baby comes, you'll get even busier. I don't know if preschool will be any fun at all and maybe I won't make any friends, but I think I want to go. You know, so you can do all your chores while I am gone."

Timidly Leah looked up into my eyes and I saw the twinkle of excitement. I saw the twinkle of a little bit of freedom that belonged only to her. Her very own adventure that she didn't have to share with anyone.

"Oh honey, that is a sweet thought for me to be able to get all my chores done while you are at preschool, but that would never happen because chores are just ongoing. And don't you worry about another baby. I will always have time for all of you. However, if you really want to try it then I will see what your dad has to say tonight. I want you to know though that you won't hurt my feelings if you love it and you don't have to stay if you hate it. Deal?"

"Deal," Leah agreed as she threw her arms around my neck.

Looking very serious and grabbing her pencil, Leah stated, "I better get back to work. Maybe they have already learned their numbers!"

***

"Honestly, I don't know what to think. Just as I was thinking God was going to tell me to homeschool, Vera calls. And Leah wants to go. Is this really God's plan or am I falling for a detour? We are several months into school already, so she really won't get a whole year of preschool, but I'm ok with that right now. What do you think?"

Sitting on the couch, holding my feet in his lap Matt said, "Well, I agree it's hard to tell. She will only go three mornings a week, right?"

I nodded.

"Well then, I think we let her go. We will know pretty quick if she hates it and if she doesn't learn anything then maybe she will make some friends. I'm ok with this if you are ok."

"Yes, I think I am. If we ever decide to homeschool I think Leah will want to have known what the public side was like so she never feels like she was missing something."

"Ok, then in the meantime I think we continue to pray and ask for answers and God will continue to guide our path."

Chapter 15

The rat race began. Amidst the hot days of Arizona's autumn Leah joined a small preschool located in the teacher's home with seven other children. Mondays, Tuesdays, and Thursdays were our busiest days. After dropping Sam off at school at 7:20 a.m. I quickly fed Grace in the car and headed over to preschool for an 8:00 a.m. start time. Grace and I would head home for chores, more eating, and Grace's morning nap and then head back to pick Leah up at noon. We had enough time to get home to eat lunch and have a little playtime before leaving to get Sam. Around 1:45 p.m. we all piled into the car again to go pickup Sam from school which released at 2:05 p.m. Keeping Grace awake was the biggest challenge and standing outside in the pickup line was equally difficult when temperatures hovered in the 90's. Wednesdays were early release days which always messed up our schedule, but we persevered. The high temperatures of autumn gave way to the cooler days leading into Christmas break and by then we were all ready for some relief from our hectic schedule.

Preschool seemed to be anticlimactic for Leah and Sam's first grade year proved easier to manage than the previous one. Sam still missed school for being sick and once one of the kids got sick, they were all sick. Since Leah was at preschool poor Grace seemed to get a double whammy of germs from both her brother and sister which allowed me to be on a first name basis with our pediatrician since we were there so often. No surprise, Leah and Grace also had symptoms of asthma which the desert air did nothing to help relieve. The baby inside me continued to grow and we all started looking forward to spring with his arrival.

***

Picking up Leah from her last day of preschool before Christmas break proved to be challenging. As all babies pick the most convenient time for diaper blowouts, Grace's set us back several minutes culminating with a complete wardrobe change. Heading down the stairs, I looked at Grace, and trying to convince myself more than her, I murmured, "Ok. Just a few minutes late, no worries."

Descending the last step, I splashed onto the hallway floor. "WHAT IN THE WORLD?"

Surveying my surroundings, I noticed that the flow of water was coming from the direction of the laundry room.

"I cannot believe this!" I exclaimed. Why does the washing machine keep leaking? And how is the dryer still on? Of course, this happens when your dad is out of town. Everything happens when he is out of town!"

Heading to the family room where the floor was still dry, I put Grace down and gave her a few toys. Hurrying back to the hall I paused to roll up my pants. Quickly splashing back down the hall into the laundry room I jumped on top of the dryer and hit the stop button. Sliding off the dryer I then turned the power off on the washing machine. Feeling the crunch of time now more than ever, I once again splashed back across the laundry room and bolted upstairs for towels. I hurriedly threw them onto the floor to stop the seeping flood, slipped my flip flops on, grabbed Grace and my purse, and ran out the front door. Once I opened the garage door and had us buckled in, off we raced to preschool.

***

"Wow, Mamma, this is a mess. What are you

going to do with all those wet towels?"

Staring down at the soaked towels and standing water on the tile floor, I said, "I am going to put them into the laundry room sink and let your dad wring them out when he gets home from his business trip tonight," I winked at Leah. "As for the rest of the water, can you help me bring in the shop vac?"

Very excited about the possibility of being able to traverse across the lake in our laundry room, Leah started to roll up her pants and announced, "Yes! I am ready!"

After we dragged in the shop vac, I vacuumed up the water while Leah entertained Grace and fed her some goldfish on the floor in the family room. Wet, tired, hungry and back aching from bending over, I plopped down on the couch and announced, "The worst is over. I think I'll wait for reinforcements to finish clean-up."

Just then the phone rang. Blowing strands of hair out of my face that had fallen out of my loose bun, I hauled myself up and answered the phone. "Hello?"

"Mrs. Smith?"

"Speaking."

"This is Maria from Desert Elementary School. We have Sam here in the office. Were you planning on picking him up from school today?"

Whipping around to look at the clock, I replied, "I'm so sorry. Time got away from me. My washing machine overflowed, and I've been busy with the shop vac. I'm so sorry. I'm on my way."

"Yes, well I'd like to remind you that all students who are not designated to be picked up by the bus are required to be picked up at the school gym no later than 2:15 p.m. It is 2:30, Mrs. Smith. I trust this won't happen again; we just don't have the staff to watch abandoned children. I'll let your son know you are on your way. You can pick him up in the office. Thank you. Goodbye."

Not really knowing whether to growl or cry, I simply hung up the phone and called to the girls, "Leah, Grace! We need to go pick up your brother."

***

Standing in the doorway of Julie's classroom while Sam and Peyton exchanged small Christmas gifts, I shared the events of my morning. "Truly Julie. A little grace. Would it have been that hard for the receptionist Nazi to show a little grace? What is wrong with people?"

"Well, you aren't the only mom who has complained about her."

"You know it's not even that she was irritated with the fact that I was late. I was late, I can own that, but it was the insinuation that I had intentionally abandoned my child; that I didn't really care enough about my child to remember that he was at school." Sitting down in a mini chair I started rubbing my eyes. "I'm just not happy with this school. I know you teach here so I shouldn't complain but I know you understand. You really are too good to teach here you know. The administration here really doesn't appreciate their teachers at all and they are getting worse about encroaching on my rights as a parent."

Breaking in, Julie said excitedly, "Oh, did you hear the superintendent's announcement about how he believed that parents really have no intrinsic rights to their child? He truly believes that the government, i.e., the Department of Education, own our children. It's the government that should decide what is good and right for your child, not the parents. I almost laid an egg when I heard that."

"You're joking, right? Is he insane? No one owns my child or his rights. God entrusted our children to our care, not the Department of Education. I'm so sorry Julie, this must make it very difficult to do your job."

"Yeah, he's getting a little difficult to work with, but most of the teachers here really try to ignore him and stick to the business of teaching which is hard enough with all the rules and regulations we have to follow now."

"Look Mom!" Sam interrupted, "Peyton gave me a Lego 3-in-1 dinosaur. This is so cool!" and off he raced back to the reading carpet where Peyton was already playing with his Lego airplane.

"Well, you really are amazing with your kids. I hope the parents truly appreciate what you do."

"I do have great parents this year which helps

a lot. So, you don't mind dropping Peyton off at the house? My parents are here so they can watch him until I get home."

"I don't mind at all, my friend. Ok, boys! Let's wrap it up. Grace needs to get home to nap. Goodness knows I need it! See you soon Julie. Merry Christmas." Giving her a quick hug, I herded the troops out the door.

Chapter 16

"I'm so sorry you all are sick again," crooned Dr. Brown. "Hopefully within the next three days after the antibiotics and steroids kick in you will be able to enjoy Christmas. Kit, you sound horrible. Have you been to your doctor?"

Coughing, instead of laughing, I replied, "Yes. And apparently, they can't do anything for me with being pregnant and all. I just have to 'suffer' through it; I think were her exact words. My OBGYN is 'watching' me but she is hesitant to give me anything unless I absolutely need it. So, I just suck on cough drops all day and sit up at night and hope this passes soon."

"Alright, well, I'm 'watching' you too. You've been sick since Thanksgiving. If you are not better after the first of the year then I think you need to see your doctor again. In the meantime, try to get some rest which I know is difficult with three sickies, but at least school is out and maybe heading to Colorado will help with some of the allergies too. As always, text me if you need anything. Drive safe and Merry Christmas.

Now, everyone give me a hug!"

"Merry Christmas to you, Dr. Brown. I'd really be lost without you."

***

"Oh you're here!!!" squealed Mom as she stood in the doorway to the house. Stepping down the front stairs with her snow boots she took Grace from my arms and covered her in kisses as she hurried inside. Looking back she called to Leah and Sam, "Hurry up you two! It's cold and I want my Christmas hugs."

Laughing, I yelled, "Good to see you too Mom!!" Carrying my purse, the diaper bag, sippy cups, coats, shoes, blankets and Leah and Sam's toys they tossed at me as they ran into the house, I slowly lugged my way inside.

"Hi there little Mamma," my dad greeted me scooping me in for a bear hug. Dropping my load on the floor, I folded into the hug.

"Hi Daddy. It's good to see you."

"You too. Your mom's been fretting all day.

Were the roads ok? How was the pass over Telluride?"

"The roads were actually not too bad. The pass had snowpack which was nice. Sam threw up at Denny's in Cortez though. Poor kid was so hungry but because he is so congested, he started coughing so hard that he threw up all over the table and everyone's plates of food. It kind of ruined dinner for everyone and after that we just got the impression that the whole building was holding their breath waiting for us to leave. So, I know it's late, but the kids might want a snack before bed."

Concern and understanding in his eyes, Dad replied, "Well, once is an improvement from last time, right? At least he didn't throw up in the car too. You go sit down now, and I'll help Matt unload the rest of the car." Kissing my cheek, he headed out the door.

"Mamma, look! Nana got another singing snowman this year. And look at her pretty tree? Oh, it's just so magical, Nana. I just love Christmas!" announced Leah, twirling with her arms extended.

"Is that a new ornament Nana?" Sam asked

pointing to Mom's 'historical tree' in the hallway.

"It is. You are so observant Sam. I picked that up when we were at the Desert Museum with you guys in October. I'm just fascinated by those javelinas of yours and how they ate all those pumpkins we set out at Halloween on your doorstep."

"I think they are so creepy, and weird looking. Just plain ugly actually. And the way they snort!" Laughing, Leah and Sam started snorting at each other.

"Hey Mom?" Sam asked.

"Yes, honey?"

"I'm kind of hungry. Can we have a snack before we go to bed?"

"Absolutely my sweet babies," Nana interjected. "Why don't you come with me while your mom gets Grace to bed?"

"Thanks Mom."

"Take your time dear. You look tired."

"I'm just weary. Just real weary."

***

"Homeschool huh? Sounds like a big undertaking honey. Are you sure you would have the time for it?" asked Dad.

"Well, I haven't decided to do anything really. Matt and I have just talked about it and my friend, Sally, has shown me some of the early curriculum she has used. Other than that, we are just praying for answers. This year has been a little easier on Sam, but he is still sick a lot and once he gets sick it seems inevitable that Leah and Grace will get sick too. I feel like I'm climbing a hill with no end in sight. I know, you are going to tell me that this stage won't last forever and I know that, but I feel like no one else in Sam's class deals with this. Peyton, Sam's friend, is never sick. It just feels like Sam's teachers, Principal, school nurse, and even his classmates question the validity of his sickness. I have even started sending him to school when he is sick and coughing and hacking but I still get questioned. And you know what really rubs me the wrong way, is that there are thirty kids in his class. Thirty! I don't care if you are superwoman, there is no way that thirty kids are actually being taught on a consistent daily basis. So, it makes me wonder, what's the big deal about him missing school? The reality is I don't really think he misses anything."

"Oh I'm sure that no one truly questions whether your kids are sick. I mean, all you have to do is look at them."

"Totally agree Mom, but the Sunday before we left for Christmas one of the boys that goes to school with Sam stopped to talk to me at church while I was helping to set up children's ministry. He asked where Sam was and I told him that he was at home sick with his sisters. Do you know what he said to me? I still can't believe it. He said, and I quote, 'My mom says that your kids really aren't sick that often. She says it's just because you don't want to bring them to church,' end quote."

"Oh my goodness." Mom said.

"I agree that's a little rude, but maybe he heard his mom wrong?" Dad offered.

"I don't know, but it really hurt my feelings, you know? I really thought his mom and I were friends. Now all I do is wonder who else at the church doesn't take me seriously."

"How would homeschooling help with that though? Do you think the kids won't get sick as often if you keep them home?" Mom asked.

"Honestly I have no idea. I know they can come into contact with germs just about anywhere, but it sure would help if parents would not send their snotty nosed kids to school that they drugged up with Advil or Tylenol beforehand, so they didn't have to miss a day of work. I realize I'm just a stay-at-home mom and I don't have a big important job with some big fancy company with only a limited amount of sick and vacations days available to use, but it doesn't matter. It shuts down our lives for weeks at a time. Even though they complain about having to take vacation time, I don't see them staying home during fall break, spring break, or any other break in between. While they are vacationing in Disneyland or at the beach, I'm at the doctor. I'm sorry, I guess I'm just in the mood to complain. I'll stop now."

"It's ok, honey. We understand. It will get better. You just hang in there. School will be over before you know it and then maybe next year will be even better."

"I don't know, Mom. I just feel like something big is going to happen. I feel like God is on the move and working behind the scenes and I'm waiting behind the curtain until He's ready to show me His plans. It's hard to be patient and to wait. I know His plans are perfect, but it would be nice if He would hurry up and share them with me."

Patting my hand, Dad replied, "In due time. If you feel Him moving then you just wait for it. I guarantee that when God does move, it will be worth the wait."

Chapter 17

And just like that Christmas was over and the rhythm of life returned. Leah continued to attend preschool, but she stated most days that she wished they would learn more things. When I asked her what kinds of things she wanted to learn, her answer was always, "I don't know, Mamma, just things!"

***

As spring arrived in the desert, so did the windstorms which wreaked havoc on the kids' asthma. The air was so dense with dirt some days that you couldn't see the houses just off the street you were driving on. It was like walking and driving in soup. Leah announced one day driving home from preschool that she sure wished God would quit vacuuming the desert so maybe the dirt would stay down on the ground where it belonged. Spring was always a hard time of year, but with baby William due soon we all had something to look forward to. Having been home bound for a few days we were all in need of a little outing and the grocery seemed like the perfect escape.

"Are you sure you feel ok to go to the grocery store Sam? You are still coughing pretty hard."

"Since you gave me that Advil I'm starting to feel a bit better. I'm kinda tired of being home actually, so can we just go and I'll lay down and rest when Grace goes down for a nap."

"Alright. Then let's get our shopping done quickly."

***

Having spent too long waiting for service at the deli and then walking around for thirty minutes trying to find the gluten free bread which they moved during the remodel, we finally got in line at checkout. In front of us was another mom with her four children. Trying to mentally figure out how old her kids were, the cashier answered my question for me.

"Well, hi cutie. How old are you?" the cashier asked the little girl who was helping unload the groceries onto the conveyer belt.

"I'm seven. And tomorrow is my birthday so we are buying supplies to make my birthday cake."

"That is very exciting. What kind of cake are you making?"

"Chocolate. That's my favorite. My mom makes it from scratch. It's the best. Right Mom?"

"Well, I don't know about the best, but we sure do like it." The mom replied.

"That is my favorite flavor too. You can never go wrong with chocolate, I say. So, did I miss something? Is there no school today?" the cashier asked.

"Oh, we homeschool. So school is pretty much every day." Replied the little girl.

"Ohhhh. You homeschool," quipped the cashier. "So, do you know what two times four is?"

A little surprised by the cashier's question when they were having such a lovely conversation about chocolate cake, the little girl hesitated to answer her question.

"It's ok if you haven't been taught that yet.

My granddaughter is just about your age and she is in second grade and she knows her multiplication tables through the fives." She glanced at the little girl's mom over the top of her reader glasses and said, "She goes to Coyote Ridge Elementary School."

"The answer is eight, the little girl blurted out. I know how to multiply." All congeniality gone, the little girl looked at her mom and said, "I'm going to sit on the bench over there and wait for you. Come on Martha. You can sit with me."

And off the little girl marched with her sister (I presume) and waited for her mother. The clerk, not really recognizing the curt tone of the little girl, proceeded to brag about her granddaughter. When the groceries were all bagged and the mother had paid, the cashier wished them a good day and the little homeschool girl was forgotten. Wondering if being quizzed at the grocery store happens a lot, I started to unload my groceries onto the conveyer belt.

"Well, hello young man. How are you today?" the cashier asked.

"Just fine, thank you."

"You are the second child I've seen this morning who is not in school. Do you not have school today?"

Sam answered, "I do have school today, but I'm home sick. We needed some more medicine."

"Oh, now that's too bad. I hope you feel better real soon so you can get back to class."

"Thank you," Sam replied.

"Well, I say, there has been just a terrible amount of sickness going on lately. Just last week I told my daughter......"

As the cashier continued to talk, I just stared. Why didn't she ask Sam a math question? Are you kidding me? I suddenly felt very offended on behalf of the homeschool mom. I wondered if that happened to her often. Did all homeschool kids get quizzed and questioned if they weren't in school? Did the mom have to carry some sort of proof with her at all times in case she got questioned? What would have happened if the poor child had not known the answer? Would the cashier have reported her? Would the mom have gotten in trouble? Suddenly I wanted to run out of the store and tell that mom that I thought she was doing a great job even though I had no idea who she was or if she really was doing a great job. Even stranger and a little distressing was that suddenly, I wanted to be like her.

***

Sitting and waiting for the girls to be done with dance class, I asked Sally, "So, does Emily gets interrogated like that little girl? Has that ever happened to you?"

"Yes, it has happened but not as often as you are thinking it does. And before you ask, yes, it really got under my skin the first time it happened. Unfortunately, there is not much you can do to change people's minds about homeschooling. That's why we don't go out and about much during the day because it's just easier to not deal with people's scrutiny and judgment."

"I'm sorry Sally. I'm sorry for all the idiots and ignorant people of the world who are married to an educational institution that fails children on a daily basis and purports to own the children of the world. I'm in that system right now and I have to say that I am truly embarrassed by them. I just can't understand why in the world that woman thought she had the right to question a homeschooler but not the publicly educated child. Such hypocrisy. I mean the outright disdain and indignation of her when she found out the child was homeschooled. Her disgust was written on her face. But you know what? The mom's face was cool. She was calm and didn't get upset. I was in awe of her actually. I really have no idea how I would have reacted but based upon how offended I was, and it wasn't even my child, I'm afraid I would have handled it poorly."

"Thank you. It's ok, though. Homeschooling rights have come a long way since it started. But people who think that kids don't learn anything or worse get locked up and abused create an environment that is dangerous to homeschoolers. That's why most of us belong to HSLDA, an organization that protects the rights of homeschoolers everywhere."

"I haven't looked at the rules to homeschool in our state or any other state for that matter, but I'm certainly grateful for HSLDA. Parents should be able to decide how to educate their children, whether it be public, private, charter, or homeschool. Who cares as long as the integrity of education is upheld and a lifelong thirst for knowledge is instilled. Wow! There I go preachin' again. Hey, it looks like the girls are done. I need to hurry home for lunch before I get Sam."

"Hi Mamma!! We had such fun today!" Leah exclaimed.

"That's great honey. Say goodbye to Emily. I'm sorry but we have to get home quickly before we turn around to go get Sam."

All evidence of happiness gone, Leah turned to Emily and said, "Bye. I have to hurry home again."

"Bye Leah!"

"Thanks for the talk Sally. See you soon."

Leaning over for a quick hug with Grace on my hip, and then hurrying out the gym doors, Leah looked up at me and said, "I sure do wish one of these days we won't always be in a hurry."

***

Walking back to the car after picking up Sam, I said, "It sure is hot today. It's only March and the temperatures are in the 90's again. Not sure what that means for summer."

"But at least today the wind is not blowing Mom. That's something to be thankful for."

Ruffling Sam's hair, I agree, "You are right. We should count our blessings. Ok, everybody in."

Rubbing noses with Grace as I buckled her into her car seat I thought about Sam's comment. Blessings. I need to count my blessings more often. So, right now, I am thankful for my kids, my husband, my husband's job, school, and even this old car, I thought. Glancing into the backseat to make sure everyone was ready for 'take off,' I hit the button on the inside of the van to close the door and turned for the driver's door. Nothing happened. Stopping and turning around I pushed the button again in case I hadn't pushed it hard enough the first time. Nothing.

"What's wrong with the car Mamma?" Leah asked.

"I don't know honey. The door doesn't want to close. Let me try turning the car off and then on again."

Nothing. Trying not to panic and starting to get uncomfortably hot standing outside on the black top of the parking lot, I waved and smiled to a few moms I knew as they were leaving the lot. No need to bring attention to my crisis. I'm sure this is just a silly problem. Again, I turned the car off and back on. Nothing.

"Mamma, I'm hot." Leah announced.

"Me too." Agreed Sam.

"I'm sorry guys. It's really no cooler where I'm standing. I'm not sure what to do. I'm guessing it is illegal to drive home with the passenger side of a van wide open."

Repetitiously hitting the button, I started to wonder how we really were going to get home. I suppose we can walk, but that is a long way for everyone. Come on car! Work!!

"We could call Daddy," suggested Leah.

Rolling his eyes, Sam replied all knowingly, "Well, we could, but he won't answer. Remember? Dad has to keep his phone in a secure locker at the office, so he won't have a clue we are trying to reach him. We are pretty much on our own," Sam stated matter-of-factly with his arms folded across his chest. Cocking his head and raising his eyebrows, he continued, "Mom could call AAA, but we would be waiting a long time for them to come and even then, they wouldn't be able to take us anywhere, just the car."

Staring at Sam and wondering how he became so grown up, Leah interjected.

"Oh. Well, that's ok. Mamma knows what to do," Leah smiled at me confidently.

Just then Grace started to fuss. Her bangs had become plastered to her forehead and little beads of sweat were forming on her nose. Good heavens I have no idea what to do!! *Please God, shut the door!* I prayed as I started to hit the button with greater intensity.

DING, DING, DING.... The door started to close.

"Thank you, Jesus, !!!" I exclaimed.

"See, told you Mamma could do it" Leah looked slyly at Sam.

"Yes, but why is the door still beeping?" Sam asked.

"Um, I don't know. I really do not want to open it again and try to close it to get rid of the beeping. What happens if the door won't shut again? I guess we should just hurry home and deal with the beeping."

Jumping into the driver's seat, I buckled my seat belt, blasted the air conditioning, and drove out of an empty parking lot.

DING,   DING,   DING...

ALL   THE   WAY   HOME.

Chapter 18

Sipping coffee and sitting on the back porch, I looked at Matt and asked, "So, you just disconnected the wire to the door?"

"That's what the dealership told me to do. They said it really wasn't worth fixing considering how old the vehicle is. So, now we have a manual door. Shouldn't be too bad. At least the incessant dinging has stopped."

"Cheers to that! We really should keep an eye out for a better car though. I really don't want to be stuck out in the desert with four kids waiting for a tow truck and a ride home. A more reliable car would be great."

"I agree. Maybe we can look next week. However, you should really get ready to go to church. I went last week so this week is your turn. I promise to watch Grace's fever and text you if I have any questions."

"Ok. I really hate not being able to go to church as a family. I'm so tired of them being sick. I just wanted to cry when they all started running a fever within hours of each other last night. I just really don't know how to get off the sick wheel."

"It does seem as if we are the only family that is constantly sick, but I'm sure it's not true. This will get better. It has to."

***

Sitting in the sanctuary waiting for the service to begin and feeling a little bit sorry for myself, I looked up to see my friend Mary heading toward me.

"Hi Mary. How are you this morning?"

"Good morning Kit," she said as she gave me a quick hug and then sat down.

"I'm ok. Chuck is working this morning so I'm here alone. He's filling in for someone today so it's been kind of lonely the last few days. I see all these families and I just truly ache for my own. It's so hard waiting on God. I feel like I need extra prayers today. I didn't get pregnant again this month and I don't know how much longer I can keep being disappointed."

"Oh, Mary. I'm sorry. God's working things

out in your favor and in his own time. Hang in there. Sorry, that just sounds so cliché. I will pray extra prayers for you."

"Thanks. How are the kids? Where is Matt?"

"Matt is at home with the kids. They all started running fevers within hours of each other last night. I'm just weary Mary."

"Oh, I'm sure you are! It seems like they just got over being sick." Mary squeezed my hand and said, "I'll pray extra for you too."

The worship music started, and Mary and I stood to sing our praises.

"Good morning everyone!" Pastor Jack greeted the congregation after the last song ended. "This morning we are going to do things a little differently. As I was preparing for church this morning God spoke to me and revealed to me that we as a church body have some needs that require special attention. So here is what we are going to do. I want you all to imagine that Jesus is physically here with us today. He is standing right here next to me and is inviting you to come and lay your burdens at his feet. He wants you to come to the altar and lift up your prayers.

Come to Jesus my friends. Come."

Pastor Jack stepped back a little and lowered the mic. I had no idea what to do. I had never been asked to do this before. I certainly didn't want to be called on like in math class! Just as I was trying to hunker down into my seat so I wouldn't be noticed, Mary grabbed my hand.

"Come pray with me," she said as she stood up expecting me to follow her.

Yelling in my head, *What? Why? Where are we going?* Instead, I found myself calmly responding, "Ok," and following with childlike trust.

Down the sanctuary steps we climbed and as we reached the bottom, looking up to the altar, Pastor Jack extended his hand and helped us up the steps. Mary took my hand in hers and gently brought me down with her to kneel before the cross. As I knelt, I noticed people all around the stage, either alone, in couples or several people together, kneeling in whispered prayer. I turned to face Mary and noticed that she had laid her forehead on the ground. Following her lead, I placed my head next to hers and listened as she prayed,

…. for me.

"Dear Jesus, I lift up Kit and her sweet family to you today. I ask that you bless them with health. We know that you know how they have been struggling with illness and we ask that you heal them Lord. I also ask for discernment for Kit as she struggles to make decisions about how to educate her children Lord, your children that you have entrusted to her and Matt. Thank you, Lord for the gift of her family to my life and to this church. Protect them, provide for them, and heal them."

Just as I knew Mary was done praying for me and it was now my turn, I also knew what to ask for.

"Dear Jesus, thank you for hearing our prayers today and everyday Lord. Today I come for my friend, Mary, and her husband, Chuck. Lord I ask that you give them the blessing of children, whether it be their own or through adoption Lord, I ask that you provide that beautiful gift. We know that you are working in your own time and I ask that you bless this family in a mighty way Lord to show this community how great the God is that we serve. Thank you, Lord for loving us and protecting us. It is in Jesus' name that we pray. Amen."

Chapter 19

"I'm telling you Matt, it was the craziest service I've ever been to. The altar was crowded, and people were waiting in lines for their turn. Oh my goodness, I feel so alive and positive. Everything is going to be fantastic! I wish you could have been there so we could have prayed together but I really think God wanted Mary and I together, today. Just us." I took a breath as it seemed that my air was running low. Instinctively I put my hand to my back and asked, "So how did this morning go?"

Standing at the sink washing the dishes from the late morning snack, Matt responded, "Pretty good actually. Grace took a nap about ten o'clock. She only slept for an hour but her attitude was much improved. Leah and Sam just spent the morning watching cartoons and laying around. They are upstairs playing right now, but we will see how long that lasts. They have all been a little cranky. Say, you look a little pale. Are you alright?"

"Yeah, I just feel a little light-headed. Maybe I just need lunch, but nothing really sounds good. Do we have any lunchmeat? Maybe

I'll have one of my 'everything' sandwiches."

Looking down at my plate the smells of my sandwich started to turn my stomach. "Maybe I'll go lie down for a bit. I don't know what is wrong with me."

Tossing and turning around, trying to get comfortable I decided resting was a losing battle. *I'm actually a little achy*, I thought to myself. *I hope I'm not coming down with whatever the kids have.* Sitting up and scooting to the side of the bed I slowly stood up. Just as my feet hit the floor, so did my water.

"Matt?! I think I need your help," I yelled.

***

Ten hours and an emergency c-section later, William Smith arrived; four weeks early. To say we were not really prepared would be an understatement considering the other kids were always born late, but my parents took the news in stride, packed their bags and started their journey south earlier than planned. Matt took a week off so he could help take Leah and Sam to school and Leah to dance and announced at the end of the week that we needed to do something about the schedule because it was just too crazy.

William couldn't have received more attention if he had been the first grandchild. Leah wanted to "help" with the baby all the time and Sam felt the need to "monitor" her and keep Grace at a safe distance. He told the girls on several occasions how fragile babies were and they should all remember to be very careful with baby William. Leah, of course, just rolled her eyes at Sam and his sage advice while Grace just nodded her head with her big eyes adoring Sam's every move. And I couldn't help but notice how very proud Sam was to be a big brother to a brother.

After two weeks of helping with baby William and loving on their grandkids, my parents went home with a car full of handmade gifts to treasure.

William turned eight weeks as we approached the final weeks of school. Busy with end of the year parties and a newborn, I prayed fervently that everyone's health would hold. But two days before the last day of school, Grace came down with a nasty cold.

"Morning Mom. Um, are you still going to bring food for my class party today?"

"Yes, honey. I'll make the mac-n-cheese when I get home from taking you to school this morning and during William's nap. We should be back at the school by 11:00 a.m. to help your teacher set up and organize all the food. I'll keep Grace in her stroller and tell any of your classmates who come near to stay away because she is sick. She probably will want to be held the whole time anyway. But after the party we need to go because I don't want Grace to miss her nap."

"Awesome. Thanks Mom!"

***

Sometimes promises are so hard to keep but I arrived at the school at 11:05 a.m. with Leah, pushing her own small stroller with the crockpot of mac-n-cheese strapped into the seat. I was pushing the double stroller one handed with William latched in happily and Grace riding on my hip. The first-grade end of the year school party looked more like a child frat party with kids getting "drunk" on sugar, carbohydrates, and multiple varieties of food dyes and artificial flavors. William sat mesmerized in the car seat most of the time and refrained from crying since the noise of the first graders was entertainment enough. Leah had fun hanging out with the big kids, but Grace seemed to get more and more irritable. Not usually worried about the health of other children since my kids were usually the recipients of their germs, I actually started to wonder if we needed to go home early. However, being good troopers, we hung in to the bitter end but by the time we all piled into the car we were exhausted, hot, and cranky. Everyone was quiet having used all their words for the day during the party except Grace. It was obvious she did not feel good and she was letting everyone know it. My only goal was to get her home and try and get her down for a nap.

By the next morning Grace's temperature was 102 degrees so off we marched to the doctor.

"She is really congested, a little wheezy, and has a double ear infection. The doctor gave us an antibiotic so hopefully she will start to feel better soon," I updated my mom as I balanced the phone against my shoulder and ear while pacing back and forth with Grace on my hip.

"I'm sorry honey," my mom sympathized

over the phone. "That is no way to start summer break. Did you get the kids signed up for swim lessons yet?"

"Oh, don't get me started on that. I don't remember swim lessons operating like a factory. There are about 12-15 kids in each class with each lesson lasting 30 minutes. How much can they possibly learn with one instructor and a bunch of kids that can't swim? I don't really think it's worth it. Plus, because swim lessons are so popular and are only offered for two weeks, sign-ups are a first come, first serve basis. So, as I understand it, I would have to go stand in line starting at 7:00 a.m. and wait until registration opened at 11:00 a.m. and hope that by the time I got to the front of the line there would be room left for the age group I was standing in line for. If you have multiple kids to sign up, then your only option is to have multiple people standing in the various age group lines. Seriously who came up with this idea? It used to be so simple. So, I guess we will just work with the kids ourselves."

"That is the most complicated system of swim lessons I have ever heard of. Well maybe next year will be different. You've got time. Plus, Sam and Leah are fast learners so I'm sure they will pick up the basics from you and Matt quickly. Keep me posted on how Grace is doing and let me know what your travel plans are for the summer. I love you honey."

"I love you too Mom. Bye."

Chapter 20

"Grace's fever just won't come down. She's been on antibiotics since Thursday of last week, but this morning when I took her temperature it was 103 degrees."

"Dr. Brown really doesn't have anything open this morning. Can you hold on a second while I go talk to her?"

"Sure. Thanks."

Before I could swallow my coffee, the receptionist was back on the phone.

"Dr. Brown wants to see you now."

"Oh. Like, right now?"

"Yes, she said to tell you to get here as soon as you can, and she will see you immediately."

"Ok. I'll be there soon."

Starting to get a little concerned, I called to Sam and Leah to get ready because we were heading to the doctor. Amidst some groans their attitude improved when I told them to pack their Cheerios and get travel coffee mugs to take their juice in. Having made it seem like an adventure I gathered up what I needed for William and Grace. Not having brushed my teeth yet, I sped upstairs, brushed my teeth, washed my face, put my hair in a ponytail and changed out of my pajamas. Within 10 minutes we were out the door and on our way to the doctor.

"I really don't like the way she sounds, Kit." Dr. Brown looked at me, her forehead crinkling with concern. Handing me her stethoscope, she asked, "Do you want to listen? It's sounds crackly like a bad telephone connection."

Listening to my daughter's chest, Sam spoke up and asked, "Can I listen Dr. Brown?"

"Real quick, honey." While Sam listened Dr. Brown turned to me and said, "I'm concerned she has pneumonia. I'm going to send an x-ray order over to the Radiology Center. After you are done getting an x-ray, I want you to come back here."

"Ok. Any idea how long it will be?"

"No, but if I were you, I'd pack a lunch."

Three weary hours later we were back in Dr. Brown's office. William was done and Grace was downright miserable. All she wanted was me. I finally resorted to letting Sam hold William and feed him with a bottle. Leah was trying her best to console Grace, but she was really too sick to notice. Finally, Dr. Brown's nurse called us back into an examination room. When Dr. Brown came in, she did not look pleased.

"I'm so sorry for the wait. I was waiting on the Radiologist to call me. Apparently, they didn't understand the meaning of 'my patient is waiting, I need the results now.' Grace has pneumonia. In fact, it looks pretty bad. Three-quarters of her left lung is under water. I'm going to give her a shot of antibiotics today and we will hope we can get this under control. I'll need you to come back tomorrow at this same time for another shot. After tomorrow we will see if we need to continue with the shots or just switch to a different oral antibiotic."

Leah grabbed my hand and said, "Grace fell asleep in the shower the other day Mamma. Remember? I fell asleep in the shower too when I had pneumonia. I didn't have to get shots for my pneumonia though. Boy was I lucky! Don't worry Mamma. I got better and Grace will too. I'll hold Grace's hand while she gets a shot. Do you want me to hold your hand too?"

"Oh baby, thank you! I think that would make both of us feel much better."

Chapter 21

"Good morning. This is Kit Smith. I'm calling again this morning to let Dr. Brown know how Grace is doing. She had a pretty rough night last night. She wants to sleep but doesn't get much rest. Neither one of us are actually. Her temperature is still 102 this morning."

"I'm so sorry Mrs. Smith. Ok, hold on a sec while I go talk to Dr. Brown."

"Thanks." A few seconds later the receptionist was back again.

"Dr. Brown wants to see her this morning as soon as you can get here."

"Ok. I figured so we are ready to leave. We will be there shortly."

Packed Cheerios and coffee mug juice were starting to lose its thrill after five days but the kids instinctively knew that I was at the end of my rope and barely hanging on. William had either slept a record eight hours last night or I didn't hear him because I was in Grace's room sitting up with her. Regardless we all once again piled into the car for our journey to the doctor. Leah, the group activity leader of the bunch had packed coloring books, a few toys (that of course could be disinfected with handy wipes), books and snacks since no one knew how long we'd be gone. Walking through the doors of the doctor office, Dr. Brown's nurse greeted us and took us back to an exam room immediately.

"You know we were all hoping for better news this morning. I'm sorry she is so sick. I can't believe no one else has come down with whatever she has. Have you given her any Tylenol or Advil for her fever this morning?"

"I gave her some Tylenol about an hour ago but it just doesn't seem to offer any relief for her. I am just so thankful that everyone is well. I'm pretty sure I'd lose it right now if someone else got sick."

There was a quick rap on the door and then Dr. Brown hurried in. "So, no improvement as of this morning huh? I hear the night was pretty rough. Is she coughing up any congestion?"

"I know I'm severely sleep deprived, but she just doesn't seem better. She coughs a little and acts like it hurts but it's not at all productive. She's not really eating and getting her to drink anything is challenging. I just can't believe that after 5 days of shots she hasn't improved at all."

"Yes, I am quite concerned. Let me listen to her."

"Mamma, Grace is going to be ok, right?"

"She will be fine," interrupted Sam. He looked in my eyes and then looked back at Leah. "The doctor will fix her. Right, Dr. Brown?"

"Your kids are so amazing," Dr. Brown replied. Looking at Sam she said, "Yes, young man, the doctors will do everything they can to fix her."

Having heard the clue words, my head snapped up from resting on top of Grace's head. "Doctors?"

Sympathetic eyes met mine. "Kit, I've tried for five days to keep her out of the hospital. Both of her lungs don't sound any better and in fact I think they sound a little worse. At this point I think the best course of action is to admit her to the hospital."

Opening the door and sticking her head out, Dr. Brown called to her nurse, "Jackie?"

"Yes, Dr. Brown?"

"Get Tucson Medical Center on the line and start the admittance process for Grace so Mrs. Smith doesn't have to do that when she gets there."

Hospital. She has pneumonia. Leah had pneumonia and didn't end up in the hospital. Good grief I have to take everyone to the hospital. No, I can't. They won't let children in. I need to call Matt. Looking around the room everyone seemed to move very slowly. My head was spinning, and the voices were starting to fade away.

"Kit!" Dr. Brown grabbed my shoulders and looked in my eyes. "Are you ok?"

Snapping out of my fog, "Yes. Yes, I'm fine. Just thinking about logistics. Do I have time to go home to grab some stuff?"
"No, I prefer you didn't. Just have a friend or your husband meet you at the hospital."

Just then Jackie walked in and handed some papers to Dr. Brown. "I think Jackie has everything in order. Here is your paperwork to give to the front desk at Pediatrics. I will come and check on you later at the hospital this evening."

"Thanks Dr. Brown, see you tonight."

"Ok, guys. Let's go. I'll call your dad in the car on the way to the hospital."

"Well, we've never done this before," stated Leah.

***

"Um, hi Matt. I hope you get this message soon. I just need to tell you that we are on our way to the hospital. Dr. Brown has admitted Grace so I need you to meet me there and take the kids. Call me as soon as you get this. Thanks. Love you. Bye."

"Why does Dad never answer his phone Mamma?"

"Well, he can't take his phone into the office because of the rules of his job, so we'll just have to wait until he calls us back. I'm sure he will check his phone frequently today because he will want to know how Grace is doing."

Just as I finished my sentence, my phone rang, and everyone jumped.

"Hello?"

"Hi babe. Are you on your way to the hospital now?"

"Hi Matt. Yes, we are in the car and heading there now."

"Ok, I'll grab my laptop and head out. I should beat you there since I am closer than you are. Where should I meet you?"

"I think probably just inside the main entrance. The hospital isn't going to let the kids in any further, but I don't know."

"Ok, I'll meet you there. I love you."

"Love you too."

Thinking I should probably call my mom sooner rather than later, I asked Siri to dial her number and took a deep breath.

"Hi Mom."

"Hi honey. I was just thinking about you. How's our Grace today?"

"Well, we are on our way to the hospital. Dr. Brown is admitting her for pneumonia. It's a little surreal right now."

"Oh, dear Lord. Ok. Do you need me to come? How long will she be in the hospital? Well, that's a stupid question. You have no idea how long she will be there. Tell you what, I'll talk to Dad and see whether he wants to drive together or just have me fly out. Give that sweet baby a kiss for me."

"Thanks Mom. I will. I will call you later when I know more. Maybe you won't have to come at all, and we will be home by tomorrow night."

"Well, from your lips to God's ears. I love you."

"Love you too."

Chapter 22

"Daddy!!"

"Hi darlin'." Matt bent over and picked up Leah.

"Grace has pneumonia and has to come here. The doctors here are supposed to fix her."

Looking at me, Matt smiled. "Yes, the doctors will fix her. So how about you, Sam and William head back to the house with me for a yummy lunch and then you can help me pack a few things that mommy and Grace will need for their stay here?"

Putting Leah down, Matt walked over to me and Grace. Taking Grace from my arms he brought her to him and kissed her head. "Hi sweetheart. I love you and I'll see you soon." Handing her back to me, Matt kissed me and turned to the kids, "Ok, let's go!! See you soon. If you think of anything, just text me. Otherwise, I'll text you when I'm on my way back so you can tell me what room you are in."

"Ok," I said. "See you soon. Love you guys."

Kissing each in turn, Grace and I walked through the doors for Pediatrics.

***

"Smith. Last name Smith. Dr. Brown already called in and registered us."

"Oh, here you are. Yes, we have Grace's room all ready for you. Follow me."

"It sure is a little busy and crowded in here. Is this normal?" I asked.

"The hospital is in the middle of a remodel, so we are operating with less rooms than normal. Here we are. I know its tight, but it's the best we can do."

Completely frozen to the floor, I stared into the room we were to occupy. Chaos was ensuing in the back half of the room. A child no more than Grace's age was screaming and fighting, and the mother (at least I assume it was the mother) was trying to calm the child very loudly in Spanish while the hospital tech was trying to keep the cords and tubes from entangling or worse, ripping out of the child's arm. Slowly control was gained in the back forty, but the loud conversation continued, so

I tried to focus again on my space. A sterile crib with ridiculously high sides loomed in front of me. A hard, rigid wooden rocker sat directly to my right. The space was just large enough for me to sit with the wall on one side and the edge of the crib on the other. Seeing us move into the room, the hospital tech on the other side jerked the curtain that divided my "half" of the room from theirs.

"So, this is your half of the room. Sorry, we are a little cramped for space right now, but I think you will be comfortable here. Just have Grace undress and then put this hospital gown on her and the doctor will be here in a moment to talk to you."

Having really comprehended nothing the nurse just said, I absently said, "But my daughter doesn't sleep in a crib anymore. She sleeps in a bed. Can she have a bed instead please?"

"Oh, no. Definitely not. She will be much more comfortable in a crib. It's regulation you know. It's to keep her safe."

I just stared at her. *Safe from what?* I thought. "Well, it kinda looks like a metal baby prison. Just sayin."

Having to raise her voice above the din of the Spanish party going on in the other half of the room, and with a hint of irritation in her voice, the nurse replied curtly, "It's regulation," and walked out of the room.

Feeling a little lost and not about to put Grace in a hospital gown yet, I sat down in the rocker with Grace on my lap. In spite of the noise, she nestled into me and slowly closed her eyes. As I sat with Grace on my lap, I watched the flurry of activity in the hallway. Voices. So many voices. I heard the loud voices in Spanish and English. I heard laughter. I heard anger and frustration. I heard despair. Just then a tall woman in a lovely blouse and skirt walked into the room. She saw me sitting there and immediately turned around and walked back out. *Hmm*, I thought. *I guess she had the wrong room.* But just as suddenly as she disappeared, she reappeared with a chair and placed it in front of me and sat down. Quietly and respectfully, she introduced herself.

"Mrs. Smith? My name is Doctor Carter. I hear Grace has been admitted for pneumonia today. Can you give me a little of her history?"

"Hi Dr. Carter. Um, yes. So I guess it started about 2 weeks ago"… "and now we are here." I ended.

"Thank you. I am going to review her file and look at her x-rays. I am also going to order a set of x-rays to be taken now. Don't worry about putting Grace in a hospital gown just yet. The x-ray tech can capture the images through her shirt. So, just sit tight and someone will be here shortly to take you to x-ray."

I think 'sitting tight' is a perfect definition of how I am currently sitting, I thought, but instead I thanked her and resumed my waiting. I didn't have to wait long before Matt's head peeked into the room.

"Wow! You got here fast," I said.

"I left two hours ago."

"Time apparently flies when you are having fun," I tried to smile.

"Hi Mamma!" Leah whispered as she poked her head around the corner.

"Hi Mom!" Sam smiled from over the top of Leah's head. "Hi guys! How did you get in?"

"Well, we told our sad story to a nice old lady downstairs about how you guys needed clothes and stuff and she told us that as long as we weren't staying, we could deliver our bags to you."

Fighting back tears, "That was awful nice of that old lady," I said.

"I'll just put the bag.... Um, where do I put the bag? This place is horrendous. Isn't there a law about how many people and things can occupy one room?"

"Obviously not in this hospital," I responded. "Just put the bags by my feet against the wall. There really is no other space."

Putting the bags down, Matt kissed the top of Grace's head, being careful not to disturb her and then kissed me. "Ok, we need to get going. I think the old lady is timing us downstairs."

Just then a hospital tech marched into the room with a clipboard and stopped in front of me.

"Smith? Grace Smith?"

"Yes, that is my daughter."

"Ok, good. I'm Steve and I'll be taking you to x-ray. Follow me."

"That's our cue to leave." Matt said. "I'll call you later. Bye honey."

Grabbing my purse, I carefully stood up with Grace in my arms. "Bye guys! Love you!" and I blew them all kisses.

***

Back in my 'quarters' after x-ray I patiently waited for the doctor to reappear. Again, I didn't have to wait long before Dr. Carter came to call.

"I just looked at Grace's latest x-rays and we have decided to move her to the Pediatric ICU. Her left lung is now completely under water and we are concerned about her right lung. So, I suppose it was good that you didn't get comfortable in here since someone will be by shortly to take you to your next room. Once you are there, the ICU doctors and nurses will take over. It's been a pleasure

Mrs. Smith. Take care."

And just like that she was gone. It was starting to resemble a factory in here.

"Thank you," I whispered to an empty space. Pediatric ICU sounded bad and I had a feeling it was going to get worse.

Chapter 23

Once in PICU the next few hours became a blur. Grace donned the hospital gown, laid down in the metal baby jail and was covered up with nice warm blankets since by then she was shivering and immeasurably cranky. An IV was attempted several times which was exhausting for everyone before a second phlebotomist was called in. I was close to losing my mind since I was the one holding Grace down while they used her arm and hand as a live pin cushion. I think the angels literally rejoiced when the second phlebotomist found her vein and secured the IV. Techs and nurses came in and out with equipment and medicine. An infectious disease sign was placed on the outside of our glass sliding door and the next person to come into the room was wearing a yellow protective gown, a mask and rubber gloves, and was pulling in a large piece of equipment. Something had changed and it didn't take too long to find out what.

"Hi, my name is Greg, and I'm going to take another set of x-rays." Moving to get up and get organized to leave yet again, he stopped me. "Oh, we don't have to go anywhere ma'am. This here is a mobile x-ray machine. I'll just take her x-ray's right there in her bed where she is laying down. I'll just need you to wear this lead apron, please. Now, you aren't pregnant, are you?"

"No, I am not."

"Well, that's good now." Looking at Grace he said, Alright, little missy, you just stay comfortable and I'm gonna take some pictures, you hear?"

After the mobile x-ray unit left, I looked at my watch. 9:30 p.m. *I better call Matt and my mom to give them an update*, I thought.

At 10:30 p.m., just as I was thinking about going to brush my teeth in the bathroom which was located outside of the PICU unit and down the hall, a new doctor entered the room.

"Good evening Mrs. Smith. My name is Doctor Stuart and I have been reviewing Grace's chart. I personally don't like surprises, so I assume you don't like them either. After reviewing Grace's history and her x-rays the staff and I feel that the best course of action is to perform lung surgery in the morning. The nurses are working on the details of the surgery now so nothing is on the schedule yet, but I wanted to give you a heads up. As soon as I have everything confirmed, I will let you know. Currently though I am working to schedule Grace for surgery at 10:00 a.m. tomorrow morning. This is a relatively simple surgery, but we feel it is the only way to remove the infection from the lung. You will meet the surgery team and the lead surgeon in the morning before surgery. She is an excellent surgeon. Grace will be in good hands."

Like he would say anything different, I thought. *It's not as if he would say 'Well she's a mediocre doctor but hey, she's the best we've got so good luck!"*

Obviously not noticing the sheer shock on my face, the doctor continued the matter-of- fact description of torture.

"We will make a small incision on the left side of her chest at which point we will insert a tube about the size of a straw, maybe a little bigger, into her lung and drain the fluid out. The tube will stay inside her chest, which she will have for a few days after surgery, and be attached to a bag that will hang down on the floor as the lung continues to drain. We will also be sending the fluid to pathology to see if they can determine the cause of the infection, but at this point with all the antibiotics the fluid will probably be sterile, but nevertheless an infectious disease doctor has been assigned to your case to make sure she is not carrying an infectious disease. Oh, and we will also be testing her for Valley Fever and various other immune disorders. Because of the blood work that will be required, and the medication administered during your stay here, we are planning on placing a pic line during surgery as well. It's much easier to place a pic line in children during surgery since the line is threaded from the arm to a large vein in the chest. Now while this may sound like a lot, I want to assure you that this is a fairly standard surgery. I think I have covered everything. Do you have any questions?"

Stunned, I asked, "Questions? Um, I'm a little overwhelmed right now. In fact, I think my brain is seizing." Rubbing my forehead, I continued, "I think I need to make some phone calls."

***

"Hi Matt. I'm so glad you are still up. Doctor Stuart, (and yes, another doctor) just left... and he told me that Grace is having lung surgery tomorrow morning at 10:00 a.m."

"WHAT? Holy crap! Why?"

"It's a long story Matt. Basically she's getting worse; her left lung is completely under water and they are concerned about her right lung too. So, they are going in tomorrow to drain the lung. My head is spinning and I'm so very tired. I really should try to get some sleep before some form of medical staff returns."

"Ok, well obviously I'll be there in the morning."

"Really? Oh, that would be nice, but what are we going to do with our other kids? It's so late."

"Well, I can call someone in the morning."

"You are going to have your hands full getting ready and feeding William. I'll call Sally in the morning. She gets up early. I'll ask her if she can just come to the house."

"Let me know as soon as you get a hold of her. I'll be up early too. I can't believe this. Surgery? I'm a little freaked out. How are you doing?"

"Scared to death. Matt, she looks pretty bad."

"She will be fine. We just have to trust she will be fine."

"Ok. Hey, I see Dr. Stuart. He's coming back in, probably to confirm surgery for tomorrow. I'll see you in the morning. I'll text you the details of when Sally will be there. Love you."

After Dr. Stuart had confirmed Grace's surgery, I called Mom, but since it was an hour later there, I had to leave a message. *That will be a terrible message to wake up to in the morning, but I what choice did I have?* I thought. Who knows what else the morning will bring?

The traffic in and out of Grace's room finally slowed down. Quietly keeping watch over Grace my mind started wondering. Hospitals are weird. Nighttime doesn't seem to exist as we know it. The lights are dimmed, the door is closed, but somehow, I am aware of the life that is beating on the other side of the wall. Leaking through the glass doors of our room I hear nurses' laughter, babies crying, moms crooning. Sitting in the dark watching the world hustle through the night, nurses and techs came in and out of our room and silently did their work. Sitting next to Grace's bed, I watched her breathe. I soaked up her face. I just wanted to crawl in bed beside her and cuddle her into my arms and smell her sweet baby smell, but the nurses had raised the side bars of the crib to "protect her" at night, effectively, separating her from me. I reached through the bars and took her little hand in mine. I leaned over and rested my head on my arm, and finally closed my eyes.

Chapter 24

"Good morning sweetheart." Matt leaned over the prison bars to kiss Grace. She greeted him with a weak smile and a moan. Holding her hand, Matt turned to me. "Sally got to the house around 7:30 a.m. Mike will bring the kids over later once he gets up and heads to work. She said he got home about 4:30 a.m. and must report back at 2:00 p.m. today. Apparently, it was a busy night on the border. How did last night go?"

"Grace slept on and off and I watched the night life until I finally drifted off for a bit. I'll just be glad when this morning is over, and Grace is back in here resting." My phone started vibrating. Looking at the caller ID I looked at Matt. "It's Mom."

"Hi Mom."

"Oh, I'm so glad I got a hold of you this morning before surgery. Honey, I am so sorry. But it is going to be ok, you hear? I won't keep you long. I just wanted to let you know that your dad is booking my flight now. I'll send you the flight details. Dad is driving down. Meanwhile, just rest in God's grace ok? Let me know when she's out of surgery. We love you. Give Grace a hug and a kiss for us."

"I will Mom. I love you both too. Talk to you soon." Putting the phone down I looked at Matt. "Mom is booking a flight. She will let us know the details later. So, hopefully we only have to worry about friends watching the kids for another day until she gets here."

The rest of the early morning dragged and sped by all at the same time. Hospital staff came and went in a steady stream. The surgical team arrived to introduce themselves, explain the procedure again and answer any of our questions. And then it was time.

"Mrs. Smith?" the nurse asked as she came into the room. "We are ready to take Grace back now."

My heart literally stopped. Matt grabbed my hand. Various people flooded the room to take Grace away. I reached out to take hold of the end of the bed. "I'm coming with her."

"Yes, ma'am. You can walk with us until we get to the surgery doors." And off we went, down the hall. Grace not really knowing what was going to happen, Matt and I terrified of what could happen, slowly followed the medical team through the hospital hallways to the surgery doors. Too soon we arrived in front of the doors. The surgeon and her staff stood on all sides of the bed.

I knew that I had to say something. I looked at the surgeon and stated. "I would like to pray for her."

"That would be just fine," replied the surgeon. And everyone bowed their heads.

Matt and I held hands and one of Grace's hands.

"Dear Jesus. We come before you this day to ask for healing. We pray that you watch over Grace during surgery this morning and keep her safe. We ask that you guide the surgeon's hands while they perform a mighty work for you. Please Lord, bring Grace back to us. We pray this is Jesus' name. Amen."

The surgeon looked up and looked at me and said, "Amen."

Matt leaned over, kissed Grace. "I love you sweetie. See you soon."

I brushed Grace's hair back from her forehead, laid my hands on her cheeks, and kissed her. "I love you to the moon and back, baby. See you soon."

Then she was gone.

***

"Mr. and Mrs. Smith?" Matt and I looked up to see the surgeon standing in front of us. As we moved to stand up, she said, "Oh please, sit," and she pulled a chair over and sat down facing us. "Grace is out of surgery and doing great. She is in recovery right now, so she won't be back to her room for another hour or so. We drained quite a bit of fluid from her lung which is being sent to pathology as we speak. I also placed the PIC line. There was no other apparent damage to the lung, so we expect her to recover very well. Do you have any questions?"

"Should we wait here or back in her room?" I asked.

"You could go wait for her in her room, so you are there when she gets out of recovery. I'm sure she will be more than happy to see you."

"How long will the pathology take?" Matt asked.

"At least a couple of days. The infectious disease doctor should be in later today to speak with you and give you an idea of what to expect from here forward."

Taking a deep breath, I asked, "So we should expect to be here for at least another five days?"

The surgeon leaning forward responded, "I think that's about accurate. It could be more or less depending on how fast she recuperates, how fast we can run tests, how her numbers look, that sort of thing. Hopefully she will be moved out of PICU within the next few days but we need to determine that she is not contagious before we do that."

"Ok, well, thank you. We won't keep you any longer," I said trying to keep my emotions in check.

"Thank you for trusting me with your daughter. Good luck."

Matt and I both grabbed our phones and started texting our parents that Grace was out of surgery and all was well. Then I texted Sally to let her know too and we set off to Grace's room. True to the surgeon's word, Grace arrived an hour later.

"Your mom and dad are right here waiting for you Miss Grace. We will get you all settled here, and you can just relax and rest," the hospital tech was talking to Grace as she wheeled her into the room. "Now, Mom and Dad just to let you know Miss Grace is going to be a little groggy still so it's ok if she does a lot of sleeping this afternoon. You just sit next to her and keep her company. The nurse will be in to check on her fairly soon." Taking Grace's hand, she said, "You get better now Miss Grace. I'll see you later."

I can honestly say that I was not prepared for the condition that Grace was returned to us. Wires, cords, tubes, bags, machines were everywhere. I was afraid to touch my own child. She didn't even look like my Grace. Her face was swollen and as she looked at me with a faint smile of recognition, she was vacant. Tearfully I leaned over the prison bars and gently kissed her face and murmured words of love and encouragement to her.

Getting frustrated with the bars and not being able to be next to my daughter, I asked Matt to help me figure out how to lower the bars. Just then the nurse walked in.

"May I ask what you are doing to the bed?"

"I would like to lower the bars so I can be a little closer to my daughter. Can you help us?" I asked.

"We don't lower the bars while the patients are in the bed. It's for safety reasons."

"Yes, I am aware of the safety reasons. However, I am sitting right here. And, let's be honest, the chances of her 'falling' out of bed right now are none. So, I would like the bars to come down."

"Well, I'm not sure I can do that," the nurse replied, obviously getting flustered and not used to being challenged.

"Well, I'm telling you that you can, and if you don't, I will figure out how to lower the bars myself. One way or another, the bars are coming down so I can be closer to my daughter."

Stunned to silence the nurse just stared back at me. Finding her voice, she finally squeaked, "You do understand that if anything happens the hospital is not liable."

"The hospital will be liable for a lot more things if those bars don't come down. I'm not out to get you or the hospital in trouble. I just want to be close to my daughter. Show me how to lower and raise the bars, please. I promise that in the event I leave my daughter's side I will put the bars back up."

"Ok, but if anyone asks…"

"I'll tell them I was smart enough to figure it out all by myself. Thank you."

Chapter 25

Grace and I lived in the hospital eight days. Pathology, of course, reported negative findings. The infectious disease doctor ordered blood tests to check for Valley Fever, antibody levels and a myriad of other things. Two different types of antibiotics were administered around the clock. Respiratory technicians came in daily to literally beat on her chest to break up the congestion. Screaming and crying through the whole of thirty minutes of torture one of the nurses had the gall to state that it really shouldn't hurt that much, and chest tubes were not painful. I would have liked to slice the side of her chest open insert plastic tubing and then move it around. I'm sure she would have still concluded that it didn't hurt at all. Realizing that the hospital staff was there to make my child better didn't help the fact that we did not see eye to eye on most procedures. Multiple case managers came to visit with pockets of goodies and stories of playrooms designed just for children like Grace to go and play or read books. Day after day the case managers would come in and try to coax Grace to the hospital playland. And day after day Grace would just lay there, her eyes vacant and full of pain. Coaxing turned to threats that if she didn't get up and walk to the playroom and play then she would not be allowed to go home and that produced an even greater despondency in Grace. She wasn't eating well and she wasn't moving. So, when the chest tube finally came out the hospital staff was convinced that Grace would surely want to play with the other sick children. I was silently vehemently against this idea since most of the time all it took to get my kids sick was for another kid to simply look in their direction. The thought of a germ-infested hospital play land was anything but magical. Unfortunately, what the hospital staff did not realize was that the only magical portal that would get Grace up and moving was HOME.

The last day in PICU was exciting. Grace had finally agreed (with an insane amount of pleading from me) to get up with all her wires and tubes and walk around her hospital room with me and then sit on my lap in the rocker. I finally convinced the hospital staff that they might as well just let us paint the walls and hang pictures because Grace was never going to venture to their magical playland. Finally realizing that I knew my daughter and how she would heal they agreed to move her to a private room (so no new infections could start) on the pediatric floor for one final night and then send her home. However, just before the final orders came in the daily blood work showed that Grace was dangerously iron deficient. If her numbers didn't increase by the next morning, our stay would again be indefinite. The hospital staff being afraid that they might never get rid of me, started giving her iron and Matt and I started praying. By noon the next day her iron levels were still shaky but high enough that they agreed to release us with strict orders to continue liquid iodine supplements at home. I couldn't pack up our stuff fast enough when the final discharge orders came in. Grace was to do as much physical activity as she was capable of but not to overdo it. The hospital staff informed us that a home health nurse would meet us at the house within 30 minutes after arriving home to teach us how to administer her two antibiotics every eight and twelve hours through her PIC line. It was suggested that I sleep in the same room with her at home with a bucket next to her bed because it was highly likely that she would not get much sleep due to coughing that would begin once the congestion got looser and looser because of the medicine. I was to prepare myself for Grace to throw up mucus and clots of blood. I was also instructed to feed her whatever she wanted since she had lost thirty percent of her bodyweight.

I'm sure I looked a bit crazed leaving the hospital. Grace refused to walk so I carried her on one hip with our bags strapped around my shoulders on either side. I'm not sure I was very visible underneath all my "luggage," but I was going home, and I could fly!

Grace and I arrived home to tearful hugs and kisses. Eight days felt like years and when I set Grace down on the family room floor, she finally smiled, sat down with tears in her eyes, and said, "Home."

True to form, within thirty minutes the home health nurse arrived, and the next two weeks of our lives began.

Chapter 26

June was almost over. It felt like the last month had actually been two years and as the kids and I sat in the waiting room of the infectious disease doctor's office we were all ready for the next 'normal' month to begin.

"What is the doctor going to do today Mamma?"

"Today the PIC line comes out." I answered

"Will it hurt?" Sam asked.

"I really don't know. Probably no more than having an IV removed. It might be a little uncomfortable."

Just then, Grace looked at me and pointed to her arm, covered with a gauze arm band hiding the PIC line.

"Out," she said.

"Yes," I agreed, nodding my head. "The doctor is taking that out today."

"No ouchies," whimpered Grace.

"Just a small ouchie, honey. It won't last long."

Eyes tearing a little, Grace said, "Ok, Mamma," and she cuddled closer to me.

"Good morning crew!" the infectious disease doctor greeted us as he walked in.

"Good morning," we all responded in unison.

Laughing the doctor said, "So, are you ready to get this out of your arm, Miss Grace?"

Looking at the doctor, Grace gave him her arm and said, "All done."

***

Just as quickly as our life spiraled into chaos when Grace had pneumonia, life reorganized itself back into order when the medicine was all finished. Grace would have to see a pulmonologist regularly and probably have more tests done, but by the first of July the medical community had given us a break.

"What do you want to do for your birthday Leah?"

"Well, I was hoping to go to Nana and Papa's house. She always has the prettiest flowers, and then we can show all the people in her church that prayed for Grace how well she is doing."

"I think that is a great idea, Leah. I guess we should start preparing our packing list then. Grace will be able to rest at Nana and Papa's house and we can get out of the desert air for a while which will be lovely."

"Well by the time we get back from Colorado, we will only have two and a half weeks before school starts." Sam grumbled.

"Mamma has God talked to you about school yet?" asked Leah.

"No, He hasn't honey. So, I guess we just keep waiting until He does. Do you want to go to school with Sam in the fall?"

"I guess. I'd rather be home with you and Grace and William, but I think Sam is lonely at school too. So, I think I should go and keep Sam company at school. No one likes to be lonely."

"I think that is very noble of you Leah." I responded.

Sam just looked at me and rolled his eyes. "I'm not lonely," he said. "But I agree it would be nice to have company at school."

"Ok. It's settled then. Sam, you will start second grade and Leah you will start Kindergarten until we hear otherwise from God."

"Somehow, I'm really not that excited about this coming school year, Mom. Maybe it's because we haven't had much of a summer with Grace being sick and all. How are we going to stay well in school this year? How are we going to keep Grace or even William from getting sick? I don't want anyone to end up back in the hospital again."

"There really isn't anyway that I can guarantee that none of you will get sick this year. Germs are everywhere and we just have to learn to deal with that. We will just be extra careful to wash our hands more and do everything we can to stay healthy. God will protect us. Look how God protected us and Grace while Grace was in the hospital. We will be just fine this year."

Chapter 27

"Who has the school list?"

"I do Mamma."

"Well, it says here that the only colors you are not allowed to wear this year is black and red."

"Why is that Mamma? That's not being very nice to black and red," Leah announced indignantly.

"That is because black and red are gang colors, so the school doesn't want anyone affiliated with any gangs."

"Elementary school kids can be gang members?" asked Sam.

"Unfortunately, yes, dear. And with us being so close to the border, the gangs are even worse here. So, no black or red. That should be simple enough to find polos, jeans and khaki pants for 5 days – one for each day of the week. Let's go to the mall to get uniform clothes for you two and then Target for our school supplies."

"I can't believe my first day of kindergarten is this Monday. I think I'm excited but I'm kind of nervous too, Mamma. Do you think the kids will like me? I don't know anyone in my class. I hope I make a friend."

"The kids would be crazy not to like you. Did you know that you are my most favorite person in the whole wide world?"

"I thought I was your most favorite person in the whole wide world," challenged Sam.

Laughing, I looked into the eyes of all my kids and I said, "Each one of you is my most favorite person in the whole wide world."

"Well, that's not possible," reasoned Sam.

"Oh honey, it is very possible. My love and faith in each of you knows no bounds. Each of you is my favorite person in the whole wide world because in the whole wide world there is no one that is like each of you. Each of you is unique and special and God's miraculous creation."

"That's true, Sam. There really is no one else like me," announced Leah.

Chapter 28

BEEP, BEEP, BEEP… Oh make it stop! I thought to myself. Who in the world changed my alarm setting? Sitting up and swinging my legs over the side of the bed, I paused when I heard the frantic cries coming through the baby monitor. *Oh, no*, I sighed. *William was just up two hours ago.* My eyes bleary, I tried focusing on the clock: 4:30 a.m. This does not bode well for the first day of school, I thought. Walking down the hall I peeked into William's room and the wailing got louder. Stepping into his room and picking him up, I laid my cheek on his head. "Oh, buddy, you feel really hot. Let's go downstairs and get some medicine."

Yay! I thought sarcastically. *First day of kindergarten and second grade. I was kind of hoping for a better start to the year.*

And with that thought William puked. "Excellent," I moaned.

***

"Mom, I see Peyton, can I go play with him?"

"Yes, go ahead. We will just hang out with you. Is that ok, Leah?"

Eyes wide and staring at all the kids flooding the playground, she uttered, "Yeah. Mamma? Do I have recess with all those kids?"

"No, sweetheart. You only have recess with your grade level."

Relief flooding her face, she spotted a girl from church. "Mamma, I see Christy. Should I go talk to her?"

"I see her mom standing with her. How about we walk over together, and you can say 'hi.'"

A few minutes later the bell rang, and the mechanical wave of kids moved instinctively toward their lines specific to their class grades. Watching Sam and Peyton run across the field toward their second-grade line, Leah and I found the line where her kindergarten teacher stood holding a welcome sign. She threw her arms around me and gave me a big hug and kiss.

Leah whispered in my ear, "See you soon, Mamma. I'll be ok. Love you!"

"I love you back, baby." And with that my brave girl got in line.

"Hi, my name is Leah, what's yours?" I heard her ask the child standing in line next to her, and I walked away toward Sam's line to say goodbye. Standing and holding Grace's hand and William on my hip, I waved to Sam and Leah as they walked into the building. *This never gets easier*, I thought swallowing down tears.

***

Now instead of one line inside the gym I maneuvered through two located on opposite sides of each other. Having learned to wait until we got outside the chaos to ask any questions, we all quickly walked out of the gym into the hot sunshine. Finding ourselves in a thinning crowd by the parking lot, I asked, "So... how was the first day of school?"

"My teacher seems nice. The classroom is separate from the main building, so we have to use the outside bathroom which really creeps me out."

"Why does the bathroom creep you out?" I

asked a little concerned that there was some weirdo hanging out in the bathroom preying on little boys and then realizing I was overacting just a bit, I reined in my crazy.

"It's old for starters so the light fixtures aren't overly bright and the floor looks likes no matter how many times the janitor cleans it, it just never will be clean. But mostly it's because of the cockroaches that cover the ceiling and walls. I'm always afraid that one of them is going to drop down on my head while I'm going to the bathroom."

Coming to a complete stop in the middle of the parking lot, I grabbed Sam's hand. "Are you serious? Has this been the case the whole time you have been going to school here?" I was literally on the verge of shrieking and my crazy was starting to peek out again.

"Well, yeah, Mom. I guess it's normal to have those huge composting cockroaches. They are seriously as long and wide as your hand. I don't think it bothers anyone else. I mentioned it to Peyton, and he hadn't even noticed them until I pointed them out. I asked the teacher today if it was possible to use the bathroom in the main building and she said yes. So, that's where I'm going from now on!"

"Sam, I think that is a good idea."

"When I told the teacher I wanted to use the bathroom in the main building and then told her why she said that cockroaches have been in that bathroom for years. She said that they have tried to get rid of them but nothing has worked. She also said they would be the only things to survive a nuclear blast. Whatever that means."

"I'm sorry honey. I seriously have no words right now. I can't believe that this seems to be alright with everyone."

"Oh, and the craziest part of my day was when Mike, a kid in my class, went to pack up his backpack at the end of the day and a scorpion crawled out and into the classroom. So, our teacher reminded everyone to make sure to securely close our backpacks since, you know, they hang on hooks outside the classroom. She doesn't want anyone else ending up with scorpions or snakes inside their backpacks. I guess last year some kid had a rattlesnake climb inside his backpack. Seems a little dangerous hanging our backpacks outside, but that's what everyone does. 'That's what you do when you live in Arizona.' That's what the kids in my class say anyway."

"Well, you had a very busy first day, Sam." Turning to close the distance to our car since the heat was starting to get oppressive and William was starting to get fussy, I glanced at Leah and asked, "You have been awful quiet. How was your day?" Aware that she had been really quiet during Sam's story, I now noticed that her arms were crossed, and a scowl furrowed her brow.

"Just great," she replied grumpily.

"I'm going to go out on a limb here and guess that your day was a little challenging," I responded putting my hand under her chin and forcing her eyes to look in mine.

"No, it wasn't challenging it was terrible." Leah looked at me and big tears started to well up and spill out of her big blue eyes.

"Oh honey. Don't cry." Pulling her to me to give her a one arm hug since I had William in the other arm, I kissed her cheek. "Let me put William and Grace in the car and turn on the air conditioning and then you can tell me what happened."

While I buckled William and Grace into their car seats, Sam and Leah put their bags in the back.

"Ok, now what happened?"

"I tried to make friends Mamma, I did, but all the girls seem to have all the friends they want. So, during recess I decided to go try out the slide on the playground. It's very popular so there is always a long line. I waited patiently in line like you taught me and when it got to be my turn some mean boy pushed past me, shoved me out of his way and shouted it was his turn. I told him that I was next in line and that he should wait his turn, but instead he grabbed my ear, ripped my brand-new earring out of my ear and threw it into the sand below and then took off down the slide."

"Oh my gosh, Leah! Is your ear ok? Is it bleeding? Did that little punk rip your ear? Let me see."

Turning her to face me I noticed a little dried blood on her ear, but the ear lobe was still intact and not torn.

"No, he didn't rip my ear. I don't know how he didn't actually. All I have left of my earring is the back. No one in line even asked me if I was ok. They just kept shoving and pushing and yelling for me to go down the slide or get out of the way. So, I went down the slide and tried to look for my earring, but I couldn't find it. I'm sorry I lost my earring, Mamma."

"Oh, honey, I'm not mad that you couldn't find your earring. That little punk should be punished. Did you tell anyone what happened?"

"Yes. After I looked in the sand to try and find my earring, I went to find an aide. When I told her what happened she told me that there was nothing she could do. I even pointed out the kid who did it! She just told me to go to the bathroom and get a tissue and put some water on my ear to stop the bleeding. I'm so angry Mamma. I don't want to come back tomorrow. School stinks."

Not really knowing what to say to Leah, I just reached out and pulled her into my arms.

"I'm sorry, honey. That kid is just a mean

bully and we should pray that one day he will realize that being a mean bully is not what God wants him to be. But you know what? I am very proud of you. I'm proud that you stood up to him on the slide when he wanted to cut in line without waiting his turn. I am proud that you were brave enough to go to an aid and ask for help. And I am very proud that you did not seek revenge against him. I am very proud of you. But you have to go back to school tomorrow to learn what the teachers have to teach you and because you made a commitment to your teacher to come to class every day. She is counting on you being there. So why don't we celebrate the end of the first day of school with ice cream?"

"Yummm, ice cream," Grace shouted from her car seat.

"Yeah, that sounds pretty good right now. I'm really hot."

"Ok, then, hop in!"

After Sam and Leah got into the car and we were heading out of the parking lot, Sam looked over at Leah and said, "I'm sorry that jerk took your earring. Want me to punch him for you?"

Looking at him through the rearview mirror, I exclaimed, "SAM!!"

Laughing, Sam said, "Just kidding, Mom."

Chapter 29

"What in the world, Matt? I'm so irritated with the school and its administration that I can't even see straight. Do you think I'm overreacting about the roaches in the bathroom? And if worrying about bullying isn't enough, now I have to worry about venomous creatures ending up in Sam's backpack."

"I don't think that you are being unreasonable. The cockroaches in the bathroom are really disgusting. I'm just grateful that the teacher is allowing him to use the bathroom in the main building. I really don't understand the whole hanging backpacks outside thing either. It's really pathetic that there is not enough space in the classroom for the kids' bags. Kind of makes me wonder where all the money from our tax increase went to last year. And, bullying? I doubt there is anything to be done now, but if it happens again, I think we need to have a come to Jesus moment with the principal."

"I just don't understand any of it, Matt. And what's worse, I really don't feel like I have any power to make changes."

"Well, let's just see how the next few weeks unfold. Maybe we just had a rough start."

***

Day followed day and week followed week until the long Labor Day holiday weekend was just around the corner. We were all looking forward to some down time. *Maybe we could go hiking in Madera Canyon or drive up to Mt. Lemon*, I thought to myself as I was just getting on the interstate to get to Grace's pulmonologist's appointment. I had just handed back a snack container of goldfish to Grace when my phone rang.

"Hello?"

"Mrs. Smith?"

"Yes, this is she."

"Hi, this Maria, from Desert Elementary School." My stomach sank. "We have Sam here in the nurse's office and we need you to come pick him up. The nurse believes that he will need stitches or staples or something and therefore needs to go to Urgent Care as soon as possible."

"What? Well, of course I will come get him right away. I was just heading into town for my daughter's doctor appointment so it will take me a few minutes to turn around. What happened?"

"You will have to speak to the school nurse when you get here but the way I understand it is that he accidentally bumped the back of his head on a concrete culvert during recess. You will also want to bring a change of clothes too. His were soaked with blood so he's currently wearing clothes from the lost and found. I'll tell the nurse you are on your way. See you soon. Goodbye."

HE NEEDS A CHANGE OF CLOTHES BECAUSE HIS ARE SOAKED WITH BLOOD???? HE'S WEARING CLOTHES FROM THE LOST AND FOUND??? Trying not to panic, go bat crazy or overreact, I asked Siri to dial Matt's number.

"Hi honey. Listen, I was on my way to Grace's doctor appointment and I just got a phone call from the school. Apparently, Sam has cracked his head open, has been bleeding profusely, needs stiches or staples, and requires me to take him to Urgent Care. If you get this message, will you please meet us at the Urgent care off 1st Street? Thanks. Love you. Bye."

Taking the exit to turn back toward home, I then asked Siri to dial the doctor's number to cancel Grace's appointment.

***

Running from the parking lot with Grace and William in tow, I slammed open the doors of the school office. Maria, the receptionist jumped and grabbed her chest. "Oh, goodness, Mrs. Smith, you startled me. What are you in such a rush for?"

Not really believing her daftness, I curtly responded, "Well, you just called me and told me my son was bleeding to death and I needed to pick him up," I said as I blazed past her heading to the nurse's office.

"Mrs. Smith, you can't go back there without permission. Mrs. Smith!"

Not even bothering to knock, I bolted into the nurse's office to find Sam sitting on a chair in the corner holding a bloody shirt to his head. "I'm sorry, may I help you?"

Not really looking at her but smiling reassuringly at Sam, I responded, "Yes, I am here for my son."

Hearing my voice, Sam looked up and broke into a smile. "Hi Mom! I'm really glad you are here."

"Oh, you must be Mrs. Smith," the nurse said. "Next time you need to wait for the front desk to announce you."

Looking like a wild banshee, I turned to the nurse, "First of all, there had not better be a next time. Second, whose stupid idea was it to put concrete culverts on an elementary school playground? Like it wasn't obvious that it was only going to end in tears and sorrow. And third, no I will not wait to be announced. Last time I checked Sam is my child and I don't need permission to come see him. I'd like his clothes please. We need to leave."

Not saying a word, the nurse handed me Sam's clothes. I took his hand and we walked out. Stopping at the front desk, I looked at the receptionist and said, "I'm heading to Leah's classroom to take her home with me. Notify the authorities," and I walked out.

***

"So, what happened Sam?" I asked on the way to Urgent Care.

"It was really no big deal. Peyton and I were playing Star Wars with a group of other boys. Peyton and I were defending the ship, which was the concrete culvert, and while we were in the middle of a battle, I must have backed up too close to the culvert and I smacked my head against the edge. It's literally as tall as me. As soon as I did it, I figured something was wrong because I felt something running down the back of my neck and Peyton's eyes were huge and everyone quit talking. Peyton asked me if I was ok. I was telling myself I was ok until I touched the back of my head and it was wet. I brought my hand around to the front of my face and saw it was covered in blood. I figured I should tell someone, so Peyton walked with me to the playground aid. She kind of freaked out and darn near dragged me to the nurse's office. By then my shirt was covered in blood, my pants were ruined, and I started to cry. Then I felt stupid that I was crying, and I cried even more. I was so worried you would be mad at me."

"Oh, honey, I am not mad at you at all! I am

so relieved you are ok. I was so terrified when the office called me."

"You look really bad," announced Leah sitting and staring at him. "Will he need to get more blood Mamma?"

"No, dear. He won't need to get more blood, but he will need to get his head stitched back together." Pulling into the parking lot at Urgent Care, I saw Matt's car. Relief flooding through me, I parked next to him and turned off the car. Matt, of course not having the advantage of calming down during a 20-minute drive with a blood soaked but conscious child, raced to the door and whipped it open.

"Hi buddy! How are you doing? Wow, that is a lot of blood. You sure you are ok?"

"Hi Dad. Yeah, I'm fine. My head is starting to hurt a little, but otherwise I'm good. Would you mind getting the clothes Mom brought with her out of the back? I want to change my clothes in the bathroom before I see the doctor. I can't stand wearing some stranger's clothes. It creeps me out."

Two hours later Sam walked out with six

staples in his head. "I do not understand why Urgent Care takes so long. I'm exhausted. How are you doing Sam?"

"I'm ok. My head really hurts now. I just want to go home and get in the bathtub. I feel gross. Do I have to go to school tomorrow?"

"You know what? I think we will all just stay home."

"Me too Mamma?" asked Leah.

"You too, baby."

Chapter 30

Autumn crept forward and all the crises at school seemed to calm down. My volunteer time dwindled to nothing since it was getting too hard to keep William happy. Plus, by the time I brought in the stroller and my Mary Poppins diaper bag, we seemed to take up more space than we were welcomed to. Leah continued to complain that she spent more time with her head on her desk than learning anything. But rules were rules and in her kindergarten class if you got done with your work early then you put your head on your desk until everyone else was done. Considering three quarters of her class had trouble using scissors, the outlook for her classroom turning into Little Einsteins were slim to none. Creeping closer to Thanksgiving Leah's class still had not started to learn to read. When I shared my concerns with her teacher about the lack of reading skills being established, she commented that they would eventually get to that when the kids were ready. Because she was such a fantastic teacher, I decided to trust her and not push the issue. However, I was beginning to get more and more frustrated with "school."

Sam's experience in his class took a U-turn when the teacher assigned him "buddies" with a new kid who had been transferred from a different school for behavior issues. Sam's job was to be this kid's buddy and help him with schoolwork and in-class projects. According to Sam he spent most of his time trying to convince the kid to do the work, and then ultimately completed the work for them both so as not to get a bad grade. The new kid was definitely not pulling his weight which frustrated Sam and it seemed he was more interested in sharing with him wild stories of abuse, drugs, and alcohol than actually doing school all the while sharing his vast knowledge of profanity. Sam was turning into this kid's social worker at the ripe old age of 7; something was seriously wrong with that. I wasn't sending my kid to school to be a mentor to some delinquent. I had no problem with him being a good role model and helping the kid out but taking responsibility for him instead of the school or his parents; I had an issue with that. My prayers became more fervent and I started feeling more and more agitated and unsettled. I felt that God was absent, and I couldn't understand why he wasn't providing me with answers. And to top it off, William was sick again. I was seriously done.

***

The flood waters broke the final week of school before Thanksgiving holiday. Crawling back to bed after calming William down for the billionth time, I glanced at the clock. 4:30 a.m., the angry red clock glared back at me. I laid down and pulled the covers up to my chin. *Why am I in bed?* I thought to myself. School madness is going to start in one hour. I just put William back to bed and who knows how long he will sleep. Although weary I just couldn't turn my brain off, so I lugged my body out of bed and headed to the shower. As I was drying off and getting dressed, I started wondering why there was even school the day before Thanksgiving. I am going to drag everyone out of the house at 7:00 a.m., including a very sick seven-month-old baby, just so they can make Pilgrim hats, placemats with hand turkeys designed on top and who knows what other stupid craft just so they can bring them home where it will all end up in the trash before Christmas. Will they do any school? No. Will they learn anything? No. Is it worth my time and energy? No. My attitude sank further and further in the tank. Adding a touch of make-up so I didn't look like the walking dead, I grabbed my hair dryer to finish. Then I turned my nasty attitude toward God. Feeling like just thinking my thoughts in my head weren't good enough for God I decided that I needed to have a verbal conversation with the man in charge. Blow dryer blasting and hair flying, I began.

"I'm really at a loss Jesus. I've really come to dread school on a daily basis. I hate not being with my kids and knowing what they learn every day. I've been praying Jesus. I've been praying every day for over a year. I even went to church and got down on my hands and knees, placed my head on the ground and laid my burdens at your feet!! But my burdens didn't get lighter Lord. We ended up in the hospital. And don't get me started with school. It is such a disappointment. There has to be a better way but I just don't know what it is. I mean, seriously, are you even there? Are you listening?"

Instead of blow drying my hair, I used my hair dryer to emphasize my points to Jesus even further. "I need answers Jesus! Or, maybe you aren't capable of big answers or answers at all!"

Losing my steam, I aimed the hair dryer back toward my head. "I'm weary Lord and I need you. Where are you?"

"HOMESCHOOL."

The word floated through the air as if the very wind had whispered it. Hair rising on the back of my neck, I froze. Hair dryer now aimed at the mirror and not my head, I answered. "What? Are you serious? You wait until I have so much noise blasting around me to give me a message?" Turning off my blow dryer I plunged my world into complete silence, and I spoke into the void. "Now if I just heard what I think I just heard, you need to repeat yourself because I need to be crystal clear about what you just said." Thinking that I had completely lost my marbles because I was standing in the bathroom, with my hands on my hips and talking to the air, I waited.

"HOMESCHOOL."

Just a whisper, a thought, a breeze, a faint breath on the back of my neck. Shocked to silence I just stood there in the presence of God. And then the moment was gone, and I started breathing again. Gently placing the blow dryer on the counter, I looked up.

"Ok," was my only reply.

Walking to the bedroom as if in a trance, I picked up the phone from its cradle and dialed Matt's desk number. Glancing at the clock, the red numbers glowed, 5:30 a.m. Matt answered.

"Hi, hon. Is everything alright? You don't normally call me this early since you are getting the kids ready for school."

"Yes. Everything is ok. I just wanted to call you and tell you that we are going to homeschool our kids."

"Um, ok? That's a big decision. Should we talk about this tonight when I get home?"

"No, we don't need to talk about it. I already talked about it with God. He made it crystal clear that we should homeschool. I just wanted to call you and give you a heads up."

"Are you ok?"

Feeling happiness and freedom bubbling up from the inside, I answered, "Yeah. Actually, I'm great. He doesn't want us to pull the kids out of school until Christmas break. So, I need to use the next few weeks to figure out what we are doing at home. Wow! I have a lot to do. I'd better go, I'll talk to you tonight though!! I love you. Bye."

Not even waiting for Matt to respond, I hung up the phone and fell to my knees in complete awe of the might of my God.

Chapter 31

Dropping Leah and Sam at school, I took Grace and William and headed to Sally's house.

"Good morning sunshine. It sounds like you've had yourself a big calling."

"Oh my gosh," I exclaimed, walking through the door, sitting William on the floor, and plopping on the couch, "talk about amazing! Standing in his presence. Hearing him. I'm truly humbled. But honestly now that I've had a couple of hours to digest it, I'm starting to freak out a little. I have one month to decide on curriculum. What am I going to do and how in the world do I even decide?"

Taking my hands in hers, Sally replied, "You simply ask. You do your own homework, and you ask for His guidance. You know He will show you. So, if you are ready, let me show you what I know. Then, we can do some research together and come up with a plan."

"Thank you, my friend."

"You are welcome."

***

Some of our family freaked out a little. Most friends from school and church did not understand, but no one could really argue with the reason "God told me to," but the scrutiny and doubt were still there.

When I went to the county office to file my Notice of Intent, the secretary said, "Good luck. We will see you next year when you've changed your mind because you failed and have to put your kids back in public school."

The support was by no means overwhelming but I plowed forward knowing my purpose and trusting in God's plan. One day at a time would turn into one week at a time and ultimately one year at a time. I knew my calling was not for a season or for a few months or years. I knew God had called me to a greater purpose and a greater plan than I had ever imagined. For those that didn't get it, it was hard to explain, but I knew that time would prove my purpose. Time would show success. Time would display all for God's glory.

Chapter 32

The alarm brought me slowly out of my dream. Stretching, I rolled over and looked at the clock. The red numbers softly glowed as the sun was barely lighting the room. 5:30 a.m. Smiling, I thought, First day of school!!

EPILOGUE
Eleven years later

"Let's move people!!! I refuse to be late to my own son's high school graduation. I will leave without you if you all are not down here in 10 seconds! Ten, nine, eight,"

"Coming!!!!" Matt responded as I heard the rest of my family thundering toward the mud room. "See, we are here. No need to make threats," Matt winked at me while placing his hand on the small of my back and guiding me through the garage door. "We should have plenty of time to get there."

"Well, I want to make sure we are a little bit early in case Sam needs something. Plus, Leah wants to take pictures so she can use some of the photos for her photography class." Looking at Leah, I asked, "Do you have all the camera equipment you need?"

"I think so Mamma. Oh, and I forgot to tell you, Mr. Johnson asked me last night if I would video the ceremony so that added a little bit more equipment but that's ok since I can claim the work for my class."

"Your photography class is turning into a very

productive trade for you. We should thank your mom for suggesting that you pick a trade along with a major for college," Matt kissed the top of Leah's head and smiled at me with a twinkle in his eye.

"Well, you can thank me later. Let's go."
"I'll help carry your stuff," Grace offered.

"And I want to help you set up at the church," William announced.

$$***$$

Walking up to the front doors of the church there were a few kids hanging out in their robes and talking with their friends. They look so happy and content. *What a perfect day to celebrate our kids*, I thought to myself. Just as we walked through the doors into the entry way of the church, I saw Sam racing toward me.

Flushed and a little out of breath, Sam exhaled loudly, "Thank goodness you are here."

Placing my hand on the side of his face, trying not to be too concerned, I asked, "What's the matter Sam? Are you ok?"

Totally flustered Sam whipped his hat from behind his back and tossed it into my arms. "This! This hat refuses to stay on my head. No one else seems to be having this problem but we are starting soon, and I can't get the stupid hat to stay on my head. How am I supposed to rotate the tassel when I get my diploma if I am not wearing it?"

Seeing his utter frustration, I decided it was probably not the time to laugh. "Well, my darling son, I have just the solution for you. Located here in my Mary Poppins purse I have tools called bobby pins! I'll have you fixed up in a jiffy." Suddenly remembering the last time I had used a simple tool to fix a "huge" problem, I had to take a few extra moments to swallow down tears. I'm looking at my son, the man, but seeing my child. Lord, please give me strength, I prayed.

"Thanks Mom. I don't know why I'm nervous. I mean, it's just a ceremony. I just want everything to be perfect for you."

For me, I thought. *And here I am hoping it was perfect for him*. Trying my best not to burst out sobbing, I calmly replied, "There is nothing that could ruin this day for me. You deserve this day and this celebration."

Finishing my handiwork, I announced, "There, you are all done. Now give me a kiss and go get ready. I can see Mr. Johnson gathering the troops."

Giving me a tight hug, Sam whispered, "I love you Mom," and was off.

Replying to an empty space, I whispered, "I love you too my sweet boy."

Touching my shoulder, Leah said, "Mamma, Grace and William and I are going into the chapel to set up."

And just like that Matt and I stood alone. Taking my hand and looking straight ahead, he said, "Let's go watch our son fly."

Sitting in the chapel the graduation ceremony seemed to pass by as if I was watching a movie in slow motion while speeding through the scene on an express train. Leah was busy with her equipment and thoroughly enjoying herself as she digitally captured the day. Wisps of hair having fallen out of her bun she glanced away from her work, caught my eye and flashed me her joyful smile, eyes sparkling with excitement. William sat next to her helping and learning and probably secretly hoping something would break so he could fix it. Noticing Leah's smile, he followed her eyes to me, grinned and goofily waved before he set his attention back to his work. Grace, my basketball beauty, tall and poised, sat next to me, her arm through mine giving me quiet support. Sam, tall, handsome and thoughtful accepted his diploma with style and ease. As he moved his tassel and shook the youth pastor's hand, he found my eyes and mouthed, "Thank you." It was a perfect day. Watching the kids laugh and mingle after the graduation ceremony, I couldn't help but drive down memory lane.

Eleven years ago, we started this journey, called homeschool. Many didn't understand our decision, and some believed we would fail or tire of the experiment, and ultimately determine it was too difficult only to find ourselves back in the public-school web. All of our friends deserted us silently claiming to have nothing in common. In fact, I think some really wanted us to fail. Trusting God's call has been the most wonderful God-filled journey of my life. I have the privilege of spending everyday with my kids, learning with them, praying with them, planning with them, living life with them. Sam will start college in the fall and my life will resume at home preparing Leah, Grace and William for God's calling on their future. The Bible says, "Train up a child in the way he should go, and when he is old he will not depart from it." God called me to train up my children and He has been with me everyday on our journey.

Keep your eyes on Jesus, take a leap of faith, and you can walk on water.

■■

www.ingramcontent.com/pod-product-compliance
Lightning Source LLC
Chambersburg PA
CBHW060434180626
46817CB00007B/2807